Mr Fitzwilliam Darcy

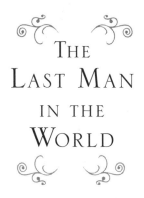

The Last Man in the World

Abigail Reynolds

sourcebooks
landmark

Published by Sourcebooks Landmark, an imprint of Sourcebooks, Inc.
P.O. Box 4410, Naperville, Illinois 60567-4410
(630) 961-3900
FAX: (630) 961-2168
www.sourcebooks.com

Originally published in 2006 by Intertidal Press, Madison, WI

Library of Congress Cataloging-in-Publication Data
Reynolds, Abigail.
  Mr. Fitzwilliam Darcy : the last man in the world / Abigail Reynolds.
    p. cm.
  1. Bennet, Elizabeth (Fictitious character)--Fiction. 2. Darcy, Fitzwilliam (Fictitious
character)--Fiction. 3. Courtship--Fiction. 4. Marriage--Fiction. 5. England--Social life
and customs--19th century--Fiction. I. Austen, Jane, 1775-1817. Pride and prejudice.
II. Title.
  PS3618.E967M7 2010
  813'.6--dc22
                              2009040358

            Printed and bound in the United States of America
            VP   10 9 8 7 6 5 4 3 2 1

Dedication

To Elaine, with many thanks
and
to Jane Austen, *sine qua non*

Chapter 1

"IN A MOMENT, WHEN we leave the trees, you will be able to see the house," said Mr. Darcy. "There it is, across the valley—Pemberley House."

Elizabeth smiled at him dutifully, then looked out the window of the carriage to where he was pointing. The house was large and handsome, even at this distance, and its situation on a rising hill above the water was lovely. Of course, she had expected as much, having heard its praises sung by Miss Bingley as well as Darcy himself. In other circumstances, she might have been delighted by it.

She became aware that his eyes were upon her awaiting her response. Obediently, she turned to him and said, "It is lovely, sir. I do not believe I have ever seen a house more fortunately situated."

His face warmed with pleasure, and Elizabeth hurriedly looked out the window again, pretending to examine the nearer aspects of the house as they drove along a stream which wound its way downhill. There was no denying the beauty of the park.

It would be some consolation to have such fine-looking grounds to wander through whenever she wished.

The driver called out to the horses as they pulled up in front of the house. Darcy stepped out immediately, then turned to offer his hand to Elizabeth. She placed her own upon it, accepting his support as she stepped down, then allowed him to bring her hand to his lips for an intimate caress.

There was no point, after all, in pretending he did not have the right or that he had not spent the previous night taking every imaginable liberty with her body. She had no reason to complain; he had been kind and gentle, but after a second long day of travel, her spirits were flagging, and she found the pretence of happiness more difficult to sustain.

He did not release her hand, and eventually she glanced up at him to find a slight smile upon his lips. "Welcome to Pemberley, Mrs. Darcy," he said with evident satisfaction.

To Elizabeth's relief, the rooms and furnishings of Pemberley House showed more restraint and true elegance than she had expected. She had tried to imagine living in an even grander and more ostentatious version of Rosings; at least her surroundings would be more pleasant than that. It demonstrated more good taste on Mr. Darcy's part than she would have anticipated. In all fairness, she had to admit there had been no reason to think he lacked taste beyond the garishness of his aunt's residence. Nothing about his appearance, from his frock coats to his horses, was ever lacking. She schooled herself to remember how little she knew this man who was her husband. It was imperative that she learn to grant him the benefit of the doubt if they were not both to be unhappy.

She was greeted respectfully by the housekeeper, Mrs. Reynolds. The household appeared to be excellently managed;

she could have no complaints in that regard. The servants were deferential without being obsequious, and Darcy appeared genuinely glad to see some of them.

Finally, he asked if she would like to see her rooms. Hoping for the chance to refresh herself, she agreed and followed him through a maze of corridors to a large, well-lit suite.

Darcy closed the door behind them and took her into his arms. It was something she had become accustomed to, and in general it no longer made her uncomfortable, but after the intimacies of the previous night, it felt like an intrusion. She would learn to bear it.

If only she could have a few minutes to herself! She had barely been out of his company since she walked into the church the previous day. It was a long time to play the role of the contented wife without an intermission.

Finally, in desperation, she suggested to him that she needed a little rest, and he reluctantly departed, promising to see her shortly at dinner. As the door closed, leaving her alone at last, her façade visibly collapsed, her shoulders slumping in despair. Surely this would become easier with time. She lay down on the bed—larger than any she had ever slept in before—to which she was supposed to welcome her new husband. Tears of loneliness and fatigue slipped down her face.

How had her life come to this? If only she had paid more attention to Darcy's puzzling behaviour when they first met and then later at Rosings, perhaps she might have prevented it. But that was useless speculation. There was nothing left but to make the best of it.

It had begun on one of her solitary rambles through the grounds of Rosings Park. It was a pleasant day; the sun was shining in a clear sky and Elizabeth enjoyed the crisp air of the morning with no hint of the disaster to come.

As had happened more than once before, she came across Mr. Darcy while passing through her favourite glade, and again, he seemed to feel it necessary to accompany her back to the parsonage. Wishing she were still alone, Elizabeth had only half-attended to his occasional forays into conversation. At one point he turned to her for a response, and with the indistinct idea he had been discussing the house at Rosings, she remarked that the house was so large she was sure she had not seen half of everything it had to offer.

"That will change on your future visits, when you will spend more of your time there," said Mr. Darcy.

His expectation that she would *wish* to know Rosings better irritated her. She said archly, "Do not wish such a fate on me, sir! I assure you that, should I visit Kent again, I will be perfectly content to spend my days at the parsonage."

"Surely you know this is no teasing matter, Miss Bennet," he said. There was an edge to his voice that made her look at him sharply.

"Mr. Darcy, I have no conception of any sort on the subject."

"You know what my hopes and wishes are," he said in a voice of tight intensity. "You have seen me struggle against it, but it will not do. None of the objections—and I know there are many—none have the power to move me any longer. My feelings will not be suppressed. I have never been so bewitched by any woman. Your low connections, the degradation which it will bring to my honoured family name, the opposition I will face from my family have long prevented me from speaking or even considering a union with someone so far my inferior."

Elizabeth's astonishment was beyond expression. Could he possibly be attempting to declare himself? *Mr. Darcy*, who was so proud as to look at her only to criticise? She could not credit it. That he would harbour such insulting thoughts about her family was not surprising, but what lunacy could bring him to say them aloud?

He continued, unaware of her silent struggle. "But ardent love will not be denied. I can no longer imagine a future without you by my side. Your wit, your charm, your beauty hold me captive. The depth of my tender regard for you can be demon-strated no better than by my overcoming such weighty obstacles to make this declaration."

She could hardly believe she was not dreaming, but she could never have dreamt a more absurd set of circumstances. She knew she must stop him, and she turned to him with great determination. "Mr. Darcy," she began, but before she could say anything further, he had taken her by the arms and pressed his lips against hers.

She felt nothing but shock that he would so violate propriety as to take a husband's prerogative. As soon as she could speak, she cried, "Mr. Darcy! You must not…"

"No, Elizabeth, indeed I must," he said in a voice of surprising tenderness. "You need not worry. I will not allow anyone in my family to be unkind to you."

"That is hardly the point, sir," she said, her voice trembling with barely suppressed anger. "You presume far too much."

"Surely you do not think your father will deny my suit?" There was a light of exhilaration in his eyes. Before Elizabeth realised what was happening, he was kissing her again. This time, she struggled free and backed away from him. She could not believe it, even of him.

His countenance expressed concern but no loss of assurance. "My apologies, dearest Elizabeth. It was not my intention to frighten you."

"Darcy!" An angry male voice interrupted them. "How *dare* you?"

Startled, Elizabeth turned to discover Colonel Fitzwilliam, breathing heavily, as if he had been running. Close behind him were two of Lady Catherine's gamekeepers.

Her first response was relief at no longer being alone with Mr. Darcy; the second was horror as she realised Colonel Fitzwilliam must have seen the entire episode. There could be no hiding her shame; there were too many witnesses.

Darcy did not even look taken aback. "You misunderstand, Fitzwilliam. Miss Bennet has just done me the honour of consenting to become my wife."

Was his pride so great that it did not occur to him she might refuse him? Elizabeth opened her mouth to deny his allegation, but before any sound could emerge, she recognised her danger. If she claimed it was not true, her reputation was ruined, regardless of whether she had welcomed his advances or not. What was her other option though—marriage to a man she heartily disliked? She looked at him, utterly furious he had put her in this position.

Colonel Fitzwilliam turned to her. "My congratulations, Miss Bennet," he said. "I wish you the best of luck with that rogue." He smiled at his own joke.

No, she was sure of it—she would prefer ruin to marriage to Mr. Darcy. Even had she liked him, his cruelty to Mr. Wickham would have convinced her against him, and she still suspected he had a hand in Jane's cruel disappointment.

Dearest Jane—what would this do to her when word of Elizabeth's shame got out? It would be the ruin of her as well, and of their other sisters; what little marital chance they had would not survive Elizabeth's disgrace. Jane and Mary, Lydia and Kitty—they would be forced to grow old together, spinsters surviving on the charity of the Gardiners and the Philipses.

Although she would not marry Mr. Darcy to save herself, neither could she condemn her sisters. Tasting the ashes of lost hopes, she said faintly, "Thank you, Colonel."

She could not even look at Darcy. He was standing closer to her than she liked, and she could hear the happiness in his voice as he accepted his cousin's congratulations. "But let us not tell Lady Catherine until I have Mr. Bennet's consent," he said. "I will ride to Hertfordshire tomorrow, and if all goes well, I will return the following day."

Elizabeth could not even begin to imagine what her father's response might be. Oh, how had she found herself in this miserable situation? Her sole consolation was that Colonel Fitzwilliam was disinclined to let her return to the parsonage with only Darcy for company after what he had witnessed earlier. She did not think she could bear it if Darcy touched her again that day.

She managed somehow to make replies when she was spoken to, but she barely knew what she was saying; her mind was awash with dismay. Surely there must be some escape from this! Perhaps if she spoke to Colonel Fitzwilliam, she could convince him to tell no one. But no, that would not help—there were still the gamekeepers, and she had no hope of keeping them silent.

They reached the parsonage at last. She did not invite them in. Darcy bowed over her hand, and when she met his eyes, she found them full of a bright fire she had never seen in him before. It unnerved her, but she forced her lips into a smile.

She went into the house, barely pausing to greet Charlotte in a civil manner before she fled to her room. Charlotte was not deceived and made haste to follow her.

"What is troubling you, Lizzy?" Charlotte asked as they reached the sanctuary of Elizabeth's room.

Under ordinary circumstances, Elizabeth preferred to keep her difficulties private, but it was pointless now. Charlotte would know what had happened soon enough; indeed, *everyone* would know.

"I am engaged to Mr. Darcy," she said in a lifeless voice.

"Eliza, my dear!" cried Charlotte. She was not completely surprised, as she had often thought Mr. Darcy interested in Elizabeth. Her friend, though, looked so unhappy that Charlotte checked her impulse to congratulate her on making a brilliant marriage and said only, "It is a very prudent match for you."

"It is not for *me* at all! He caught me quite by surprise with his proposal, and I should have refused him in no uncertain terms, but before I could, he *kissed* me without so much as a by-your-leave, and we were observed," Elizabeth said angrily. "He is the last man in the world I wish to marry."

"Oh, Lizzy. I am sorry you are unhappy about it. I know how much you dislike him, but is it not possible that with greater knowledge of him, your opinion might improve?"

"What is there to learn of him? I know what he has done to Mr. Wickham, I have heard him speak most degradingly of my family, and he has conceit enough to *assume* I would marry him!

If it were not for the disgrace it would bring my sisters, I would never, never have agreed."

"It will be an advantage for your sisters as well. Only think, you may be in a position to bring Mr. Bingley and our dear Jane back together."

"Something which is only necessary because *my* future husband likely had a hand in separating them!" Elizabeth paused to think; it would be some consolation to her if her sacrifice could lead to Jane's happiness.

Charlotte observed the change in her friend's face. "Marriage is a matter of compromise, Eliza. I know you believe I have compromised more than I ought. I do not think Mr. Darcy is totally without redeeming features, even apart from the practicalities. By all reports he is a good brother and guardian to his sister, and Colonel Fitzwilliam and Mr. Bingley, both amiable gentleman, have called him friend for years. He is well educated and sensible, which I know is of importance to you. He has his faults, but I cannot believe he is *all* bad." She left hanging between them the spectre of Mr. Collins; knowing Lizzy feelings about him, Charlotte felt perhaps the comparison might give her some ease.

Elizabeth stood and began to pace the room. "I grant you he is not completely despicable, but I do not wish to marry him!"

Charlotte did not respond for some time. Finally, she said, "No, of course you do not, but given that you must, there is nothing for it but to make the best of it. Perhaps you cannot love him, but you must work on finding things to like in him, Lizzy. Your resentment will do you nothing but harm in the end."

She could hear the sense in her friend's words, much as she disliked them. Closing her eyes tightly and clenching her fists, Elizabeth said, "So what is your advice then, Charlotte?"

"Be amiable to him, my dear. He must be violently in love with you to have made you an offer. That will naturally incline him to treat you well, if you do not give him reason to change his mind. Perhaps, at some point, your influence may be enough to lead him to alter some of those behaviours you dislike in him."

"Your advice is eminently practical," said Elizabeth, "but you know I am no actress. I cannot counterfeit well, and I confess I feel no urge to make him happy."

"I am not suggesting this in his interest but in yours. What will *your* life be like if you make him miserable? Would you live with a husband who hates you? Please, Lizzy, do not give him that power; for your own sake, find ways you can be happy within a marriage you do not want. You need not spend much time with him once you are married."

Elizabeth was not a fool; she could see her friend's point, and she spent the next day schooling herself to acceptance. It was not easy for one of her spirits. She made a list of Mr. Darcy's virtues in her mind—albeit a very short list—and repeated it to herself regularly. She could not help wishing *something* might happen— that her father might refuse his consent, though it would solve nothing, or at the very least that Darcy's return would be delayed. She did not trust her own ability to dissemble, and after the events surrounding his proposal, she was not under the illusion that he would make no physical demands during their engagement. She planned to make every effort to avoid being alone with him.

His arrival was timely, however, and brought news of Mr. Bennet's consent and a letter from him to Elizabeth. She met him with a smile and put the letter aside for later. Knowing her father, she did not expect it to contain the normal platitudes, and she did not imagine he would be happy with this match.

To her dismay, no sooner had Darcy appeared than Charlotte manufactured an excuse to leave them alone together. Glancing despairingly after her friend, Elizabeth said hurriedly, "Did you find my family well, sir?"

"Your father was well, but I confess I did not see any of the others."

"My mother was not aware of the occasion of your visit?"

"Your father kindly offered to share the intelligence with Mrs. Bennet," Darcy said in a tone of slight distaste. "I was happy to absent myself from the occasion."

I am sure you were! thought Elizabeth indignantly. *Why tolerate more degradation than necessary?* "I am glad it did not take up any more of your time," she said, trying to mask her hostility with a smile. *Remember, Bingley and Colonel Fitzwilliam think highly of him. He is truthful. He is a good brother.* The litany was becoming wearying.

"It allowed me to return to your side as soon as I could," he said with slightly more grace.

Elizabeth wondered what he had been thinking all those times he had stared at her in the past. Clearly, it was not *only* to criticise. She could not comprehend, though, how he had come to love her, for love her he must to make her an offer despite his opinion of her family. She had rarely been anything but saucy and impudent to him, and he had not often troubled himself to speak to her. Now her cheeks coloured at what he might be thinking.

He took her blush to mean something else though, and moved to the chair beside hers. Taking her hand, he pressed it to his lips.

It is only a kiss on your hand. Other gentlemen have done the same, she told herself. *There is no reason to allow it to trouble you now.* Other men, however, did not fix their eyes on her with such heated intensity, nor hold her hand a little too long. She looked away uncomfortably.

He gave a low laugh. "I would not have expected you to be shy, Elizabeth."

His use of her Christian name only fuelled her embarrassment. "Mr. Darcy, you must allow me some time to become accustomed to thinking of you as something beyond an acquaintance."

"Surely you knew I would be making my addresses."

"I assure you, sir, there was nothing in the world I expected less," she replied spiritedly. It was one thing to be pleasant to him, but there was no reason to pretend she had been part of some covert courtship process.

"I cannot believe you failed to notice my interest in you," he said. "Or did you think perhaps I was only trifling with your affections?" He sounded amused by his conceit.

"Sir, it never crossed my mind that you particularly noted my existence or thought me more than merely *tolerable*." She realised she was very close to provoking a quarrel with him and reminded herself how disadvantageous such an action would be. With a distinct effort, she smiled at him.

He looked at her probingly. "Perhaps that explains something."

Elizabeth was not at all certain she wished to know what it explained, but she responded as he evidently expected. "And what is that?" In another lifetime she might have said it archly or even chosen to tease him by ignoring his hint, but no longer.

He did not quite smile, but his eyes warmed. "I had not realised I was taking you by surprise."

She gave him a puzzled look, then her eyes grew larger as he leaned towards her, his intent obvious. He said, "Perhaps this time you will not be caught unawares."

His lips touched hers. She felt a moment of panic at the intimacy of it. She would not let it show though; instead, she forced herself to think how her marriage might provide another chance for Jane and Mr. Bingley.

Although it was distinctly odd to be kissed by Mr. Darcy, it was neither terrible nor disgusting, she decided; it was *tolerable*. The thought of applying that term to him was rather amusing. Perhaps she should start trying to think of him as tolerable.

"Yes—that is better," he said softly as he drew away.

If all he expects of me is not to push him away when he wants to kiss me, it ought to be simple enough. She would have to ask someone, perhaps her aunt Gardiner, how much more there was to marriage. The thought made her blush, which seemed to please her new husband-to-be.

Chapter 2

CHARLOTTE WAS TACTFUL ENOUGH to ask no questions after Mr. Darcy's visit, and Elizabeth took her first opportunity to escape to her room. Reading her father's letter was her first order of business, though she feared what it might contain.

I have only a moment to write to you, Lizzy, so I must speak my mind directly. Mr. Darcy has asked my permission to marry you, claiming he has your consent. I must caution you to consider carefully before you enter into this engagement. I cannot see you being happy with Mr. Darcy. Have you not always hated him? Is his wealth enough reason to tolerate a man you dislike as your husband? I know your temperament, and I cannot believe you would be truly happy unless married to a man you could esteem as your superior. Please do not give me the pain of seeing you so unhappy in your choice of a partner in life. I have given him my permission; indeed, he is not the sort of man to whom I could deny anything once he had lowered himself to ask for it, but I beg you to reconsider while there is still time. I will not tell anyone of this matter, most especially your mother, until I hear from you with your final decision.

If only she could follow his advice! Unfortunately, she had no such choice. She folded the letter carefully and placed it in her drawer, then thought better of it and took it to the fire. There was no reason to save it. She would have to dispose of any document which spoke so of Mr. Darcy soon enough, else risk his finding it. She shivered, watching the letter shrivel and turn black, thinking of the loss of privacy marriage to him would entail. *No,* she resolved, *I must not think this way. I shall merely need to learn new habits of privacy.*

It was final now. She could no longer hope for a miraculous escape. Her father had consented, and Mr. Darcy would no doubt be telling his family tonight. She smiled a little, wondering how Lady Catherine would take the knowledge of her new niece and the thwarting of her plans for her daughter. No, she did not envy Mr. Darcy that interview.

The next day, Mr. Collins returned early from his morning call at Rosings Park his face ashen and his manner agitated. Bursting into the sitting room, he insisted on immediate conference with Charlotte. Elizabeth and Maria exchanged puzzled glances as Charlotte disappeared behind her husband.

When Charlotte returned a short time later, her distress was evident. "I barely know how to say this, Lizzy, but please believe this is not my desire. Lady Catherine is beside herself with anger over your... situation," she said. "She learned of it this morning, and she apparently holds *you* wholly responsible for the ruination of all her plans. Mr. Collins, I am sorry to say, insists you leave this house immediately."

"What!" exclaimed Maria, who remained blissfully unaware of Elizabeth's engagement, as had Mr. Collins before receiving intelligence of it from Lady Catherine herself.

The news did not come as a complete surprise to Elizabeth, who had not shared Mr. Darcy's lack of concern for Lady Catherine's reaction to his announcement. Although she had not anticipated Mr. Collins would go so far as to expel her from his home, it was an outcome with certain favourable aspects for her. She had no desire to remain in Mr. Darcy's vicinity for any longer than necessary; soon enough she would have no choice in the matter but to be at his disposal.

"What, then, am I to do?" Elizabeth addressed her question to Charlotte, ignoring Maria's outburst.

"Mr. Collins has already left to make arrangements for you to take the next post to London," said Charlotte with some embarrassment. "I tried to convince him it was not in our best interests to anger Mr. Darcy, but it did no good. He is adamant. I cannot imagine what Lady Catherine said to him; perhaps it is best for you to be gone before she decides to take you to task directly. But it is hardly fitting for you to travel alone. Perhaps I should send for Mr. Darcy?"

"No," Elizabeth said quickly, "I would rather not trouble Mr. Darcy."

It was eventually decided that Maria Lucas would accompany Elizabeth to London as planned, only departing immediately instead of a week hence. Although at first Maria was sorry to be deprived of the pleasure of visits to Rosings, once she heard the details of Elizabeth's situation, she recognised there was little merit in remaining at Hunsford while the Collinses were in deep disgrace with Lady Catherine.

⁂

As the coach pulled away from Hunsford village, Elizabeth's mind turned to how she was to explain her sudden appearance to her aunt and uncle. Beyond this lay the question of how to present her engagement to them. Ought she to tell them the truth of it or present a prettier picture in which she gladly accepted his addresses?

In the end, she chose the path of caution, and told them her opinion of Mr. Darcy had undergone a change after seeing him amongst his family and of her current pleasure in their engagement. Jane was, perhaps, the most predisposed to accept this story. Having always valued Darcy herself, she required little persuasion that Lizzy might have learned to do so as well. Her aunt, whose only exposure to Darcy had been hearing about his faults from Mr. Wickham at Christmastime, was more concerned.

"But, Lizzy," said Mrs. Gardiner, "what of how infamously he treated poor Mr. Wickham? I am worried about you marrying such a man—and one you held in such disdain only a few months ago."

Elizabeth was little prepared to meet this charge and produced an incoherent answer to the effect that if Mr. Darcy were as proud as Wickham claimed, he would not be marrying *her*. Her aunt appeared dubious but ceased to press her.

Elizabeth was grateful for the respite, as she had more than enough to worry about regarding Mr. Darcy's response to her precipitate departure. She suspected he would not be happy she had left without a word. Now that they were officially engaged, there was no reason she could not have left him a note or even written to him once she reached London. But she had taken the coward's way out, and now she could not make herself put pen to paper. It was somehow less palatable to be deceptive about her feelings in writing than in person.

He would have no trouble finding her. Charlotte would be happy to tell him her destination. It was only a matter of how long he chose to wait before coming after her. Elizabeth was not looking forward to discovering what sort of temper her husband-to-be possessed or how he would react to finding himself among her low connections in Cheapside. She wondered whether he would stay the remaining days he had planned at Rosings or whether he would follow her sooner. Assuming he did not immediately discover her departure from Hunsford, the earliest she could expect to see him was the following afternoon.

She was therefore taken by surprise when the Gardiner's manservant announced Mr. Darcy's arrival the following morning. Nervously, she stood as he entered, but to her relief he looked no different from usual—rather distant and severe, but not angry. When he managed to catch her eye, he actually seemed pleased.

His response when she introduced him to her aunt was rather perfunctory. She feared this would not improve Mrs. Gardiner's opinion of him. She was grateful for her aunt's fine manners, politely asking him whether he would like some refreshment and beginning a conversation about Derbyshire. Darcy thawed a little as it became evident he was not dealing with another Mrs. Bennet, but his manner did not go so far as warmth.

Elizabeth, growing somewhat anxious as time went on as to what her aunt and Jane might be thinking, suggested to Mr. Darcy that perhaps they might walk out in order to enjoy the fine day. It was ironic, she thought, that now she was seeking to be alone with him, but it was not out of any desire for his company.

He assented readily. Elizabeth fetched her bonnet, and as soon as they were outside of the house, Darcy turned a look of great warmth on her. "Elizabeth, I am very glad to be with you again."

She blushed, remembering the kisses which had accompanied such a tone of voice from him in the past. "I had not expected you quite so soon, sir."

"I returned to town yesterday evening, but far too late to call, so I thought it better to wait until this morning. Surely you did not think I would remain at Rosings once you had left."

She was unsure what he wished her to say. "I am sorry if this has caused trouble between you and Lady Catherine."

He glanced down at her. "I do not know what you have heard, although I assume it was what prompted you to leave."

Apparently, his source at Hunsford had neglected to inform him she had no choice but to depart. She chose her words carefully. "I understood from Mr. Collins that she was quite unhappy with the news. Rather than put him in an uncomfortable position with his patroness, I thought it wisest to leave."

"You are kind to be sensible of his position, but I hope you understand that as my future wife, you need fear no one."

She wondered if he thought it below her to worry about Mr. Collins. However agreeable she planned to be to her future husband, she did not intend to behave with his sort of pride. "Mrs. Collins is a very dear friend. I would not hurt her for the world."

"Of course not." He seemed more satisfied by this explanation. "It is unfortunate your visit with her was interrupted. Have you made plans for your stay in London?"

She reminded herself of Charlotte's advice. "I am entirely at your disposal, sir. My parents do not yet know I have left Kent."

He looked at her questioningly for a moment. "It would please me if you had an opportunity to make my sister's acquaintance while you are in London."

"I would be happy to do so." Elizabeth hoped Miss Darcy was not as proud as Wickham had indicated to her.

"We need to discuss our wedding as well."

"Indeed." Elizabeth felt suddenly closed in by the people and buildings around them and had a longing for the open countryside near Longbourn. She would not be able to enjoy it long, even when she returned home. She hoped the scenery in Derbyshire would not be cold and forbidding.

"I see no reason to delay overlong. What is your view?"

"I have not given the matter any thought yet, sir." Elizabeth dropped her eyes to the dirty cobblestones beneath her feet.

"I am not minded to think that a long courtship in the presence of your family would be pleasurable to either of us. Do you think a month would be adequate planning time?"

A year would not be a long enough delay for her. "That might seem very sudden, sir."

He favoured her with a smile which transformed his features. "Would you mind that?"

Elizabeth felt a wave of panic as she sought for a way to convince him to wait longer. "Perhaps I could consult with my aunt before we decide. After all, I have never planned a wedding before."

He laughed. "Nor have I. It will be our first new experience together."

Georgiana Darcy awaited with trepidation meeting her future sister. She could not have been more astonished when her brother arrived in London unexpectedly with the announcement that he was to be married, and to a woman she had never heard of. She dared not ask him many questions, but she was concerned, especially when he described Miss Bennet as possessing an admirable spirit. Fitzwilliam's wife would have a great deal of influence on the next years of her life, arranging her coming out and no doubt having some say in her choice of husband. If Miss Bennet was wilful, Georgiana would never be able to stand up to her. She trusted Fitzwilliam with her future, but it was harder with this unknown woman.

But she would not be unknown for long. Georgiana could hear the carriage pull up in front of the townhouse. She stood and smoothed her skirts, trying to disguise her nervousness. It took longer than she expected between the time when she heard the front door open and when Fitzwilliam appeared in the doorway accompanied by a graceful young lady, not quite as tall as Georgiana herself.

"Georgiana, may I present Miss Elizabeth Bennet?"

"Miss Bennet, it is a great pleasure to make your acquaintance."

"And yours as well, Miss Darcy. I have heard so much about you. I understand you are a talented musician."

"A musician of sorts, yes, but hardly talented," said Georgiana as Fitzwilliam offered Miss Bennet a seat on the sofa.

"You are too modest, I am sure."

Fitzwilliam, who was looking at Miss Bennet with undisguised fascination, said, "Someday you will have the opportunity to hear Georgiana play, and you may judge for yourself. I venture to say you will not be disappointed."

"I shall look forward to it."

To Georgiana it did not sound as if Miss Bennet were looking forward to it in the slightest. With a sinking heart she said, "Will you be staying long in London, Miss Bennet?"

"Not long. I must return home within the week."

Fitzwilliam smiled warmly at Miss Bennet. "Elizabeth and I have just agreed on when she will make me the happiest of men. She has many preparations to make quickly, since I am impatient enough to wish to marry her next month."

Georgiana was profoundly shy, but she had no difficulty in reading character, and Miss Bennet's expression was more suited to planning a funeral than a wedding. Even her smiles at her intended looked forced. Georgiana felt almost as wretched seeing her brother so enamoured of a woman who clearly did not return his regard. Fitzwilliam had been caught by a fortune hunter after all.

Apparently, she was not to have the sister of her dreams. Georgiana reminded herself she had survived many other disappointments in her life. At least Miss Bennet was not pretending a fawning interest in her as some ladies did, hoping to curry her brother's favour. But by all appearances, Miss Bennet had no need to do anything at all to please Fitzwilliam; he was happy just looking at her.

Georgiana straightened into the proper posture so carefully taught to her at school. "Miss Bennet, may I offer you some refreshment?"

Chapter 3

"A LETTER FOR MISS Elizabeth," Hill announced.

Mr. Bennet took the sealed letter off the tray, examined it, then handed it to his second daughter. "Your young man, I daresay."

The direction was in a masculine hand, so there could be little doubt who had sent it. "Thank you, Hill," Elizabeth said.

Since her return to Longbourn a week earlier, Elizabeth had astonished herself with her ability to forget the disaster looming in her future, even when forced to listen to her mother's raptures over her upcoming marriage constantly. She did not have to tolerate Mr. Darcy's attentions; he was off to Matlock to announce their engagement to his aunt and uncle, or more precisely to soothe their vexation over learning of the news through the biased view of Lady Catherine. Without his presence, it was easier for her to pretend she was happy about this marriage, and as long as this was the general belief, no one troubled her overmuch for details. Even her father appeared to have accepted it, though upon occasion she found him looking dubiously at her. But Elizabeth could find no justification for confiding in him; there was no point in making him suffer with the knowledge of her regrets.

She spent this time as if it were the final days of summer, with the nip of evening frost warning of the winter to come, urging her to make the most of the last fine days. But someday spring would come again, she reminded herself. She would make new friends in Derbyshire, and if she had been able to tolerate life with her mother and younger sisters, surely she could learn to endure Mr. Darcy. At least *he* was quiet more often than not and would not embarrass her in public. Once she had children, he would not expect to be the center of her life. Although she preferred not to think on the begetting of her children, she would love them no matter what her opinion of their father might be.

It was more difficult to feel bold with the concrete evidence of Mr. Darcy's post in her hand. A happy bride would be delighted by a letter from her intended. She forced a smile to her lips. "If you will excuse me." She dropped a curtsey and made her way upstairs to her room.

Once there, she tossed the letter on the wash table, kicked off her slippers, and curled up in the window seat. She felt no inclination to see what Mr. Darcy had to say and instead picked up the novel she had been reading earlier. But her mind refused to focus on it, and with a sigh, she left her repose to take up the letter, eyeing it as if it were Pandora's box. It would be better to have it done with. Carefully, she broke the seal.

My dearest Elizabeth,

At last I may report to you that our separation will soon come to an end. I am writing from Matlock, where I have

*informed my aunt and uncle of our impending nuptials. I will
leave for London tomorrow, and if the weather and roads
permit, I shall be at Longbourn Monday next.*

*It has been only a week since I saw you last, but it seems
far longer since I was last delighted by your smile. You are
always in my thoughts, no matter where I may be. I wonder
what you are doing now and wish I might be there as well.
I think it will be quite some time before I am willing to part
from you again after our marriage, which cannot come too
soon for me. I wish I had the facility of words some gentlemen
possess, to tell you how dearly I miss you and of my joy in
our engagement, but since I have only my poor ability with
which to express myself, I shall close by reminding you that I
remain your ardent admirer,*

F.D.

Embarrassed and not a little ashamed, as if she had been
eavesdropping on a private conversation she had no right
to hear, Elizabeth folded the paper carefully and placed it in
her pocket. The reminder of Darcy's sentiments made her
uncomfortable; she felt almost guilty for her reluctance to marry
him. He did not deserve to be deceived into allowing himself
to express his feelings without the knowledge that she did not
share them. But what was the alternative—to ask him not to
speak words of love to her because she was marrying him against
her wishes? That would not do.

Poor man, to believe he was loved and admired where he
was not. That he held her in tender regard she did not doubt,
for he could never have overcome his objections to her family
if he had not. Why he should possess such feelings was more

puzzling. Given how impudent she had been to him during their acquaintance, it was a wonder. Was he so inexperienced in caring as to mistake *that* for love?

There was, in that moment, a more gentle sensation towards him in her mind than she had ever felt before. Though she still resented his presumption, she found something in him to pity as well.

Darcy was true to his word and arrived on the date promised. When he stepped into the sitting room at Longbourn, his eyes immediately seeking Elizabeth out with the look she was beginning to recognise was not criticism but admiration, she felt a familiar heaviness come over her. She smiled at him dutifully as she curtsied and answered all his queries with civility. She was grateful her mother stood in such awe of her intended son-in-law that she ventured not to speak to him, unless it was in her power to offer him any attention or mark her deference for his opinion. The last thing Elizabeth wished was to offer him any further confirmation of his low estimation of her family.

She was relieved when he proposed walking out, despite her suspicion it would lead to certain attentions she preferred to avoid. At least it would reduce the likelihood of scenes embarrassing to them both.

Darcy was silent as they strolled down the lane. Once they were out of sight of Longbourn, he favoured her with a smile which brought more warmth to his features than she would have once thought possible. "How I have missed you, my sweetest, loveliest Elizabeth."

The regret she had felt on reading his letter returned in force, coupled with doubt as to the correct course for her. She could not pretend to feelings she did not possess, yet neither could she ignore his words nor suggest they were unwelcome, and she did not wish to be unkind. Finally, she cast her eyes downwards and murmured, "You are welcome back to Hertfordshire, Mr. Darcy."

"What, still blushing?" His countenance bespoke amusement.

"Do you object to my blushing, sir?" she asked archly.

"I object to nothing about you, my love, except perhaps your current marital status." He took her hand and placed it on his arm.

It was difficult to listen to his endearments knowing how little she would ever be able to reciprocate them, and she once again found herself in the curious position of feeling a sort of pity for Mr. Darcy. Thus it was that when he bent to kiss her, she accepted it with more grace than she had in the past.

He must have felt the difference since he carefully drew her into his arms, never allowing their lips to part. She did not resist him and, finding no other spot to put her arms, followed her instinct and placed them around his neck. She did not realise how much more vulnerable this made her until she felt the strangeness of his body pressed against hers. It was an entirely novel sensation and, surprisingly enough, not an unpleasant one. It felt somehow natural to touch this way, and, if she did not think too hard about whose arms she was in, she could even have said she enjoyed the feeling of his arms around her.

He did not ask more of her than the gentle pressure of her lips against his, nor did he keep her in his embrace long. With an air of pleased satisfaction, he replaced her hand on his arm and began to walk again.

Elizabeth was more confused by her reactions. It was in her best interests to find his actions unobjectionable and even pleasant; why, then, should she be disturbed to find it was so? Still, when she stole an embarrassed glance at Darcy's face, she saw an expression which bespoke a new happiness on his part, and she discovered to her surprise that she was glad of it.

"How are the plans for the wedding coming along?" he asked.

"Quite well, I believe." Since Elizabeth preferred not to think about her wedding, she had ceded most of the decisions to her mother. She supposed she ought to show some sort of interest in it, so she said, "Will any of your family be in attendance?"

"Only my sister and Colonel Fitzwilliam. They will not arrive until the preceding night, since I would prefer to minimise the risk of Georgiana encountering… Meryton society."

Any small pleasure she had felt in his company vanished. She could not feel regret for her inability to love him when he was so ready to disparage her family and friends. She did not understand how he could possibly expect her to share his views; yet apparently, he did. To think she had almost enjoyed his earlier attentions!

Think of Jane, she told herself. *Think of giving her another chance with Mr. Bingley.*

Darcy was in near-constant attendance upon Elizabeth at Longbourn over the next two days. He spoke little when any of her family was present, saving his discourse for when they were alone together. Elizabeth tried to keep those occasions to a minimum; but even so, she began quickly to chafe at her lack of freedom. Finally, she suggested to Mr. Darcy that there were some few preparations she needed to make for their wedding, items she planned to purchase which she wished to be a surprise to him on their wedding day. Although she was certain anyone could have recognised this as a weak excuse, Darcy did not seem to consider it a possibility, going so far as to appear pleased she was making such an effort.

So it was he left her to herself for the afternoon. Feeling it incumbent upon her to live up to her word, Elizabeth took a lingering ramble into Meryton. She paused in each of her favourite shops, wondering when she would see these familiar streets again.

On exiting the milliner's shop Elizabeth happened upon Mr. Wickham. Her cheeks were immediately covered by the deepest blush at what he must think of her. In accepting Mr. Darcy, she must seem mercenary at best and duplicitous at worst. "Mr. Wickham," she murmured, dropping a curtsey while avoiding his eyes.

"This is an unexpected pleasure, Miss Bennet." He sounded as warm and amiable as ever. She risked a glance at him and saw no hint of disapproval. "I understand I must congratulate you."

"Thank you, sir." Though his bearing reassured her, she was less comfortable with what remained unspoken. "Although I hope you wish me well, I had not thought you, of all people, would wish to congratulate me."

An expression of concern covered his brow. "My dear Miss Elizabeth, you mistake me entirely. To me, Pemberley is the most beautiful place on earth, and I cannot imagine you will be anything but happy as the mistress of it. It is not something one could refuse."

She released her breath in relief at his respectful tone. Apparently, he bore her no ill will for her decision. Given his interest in Miss King, he must view her as making the same compromises he himself had. She wished she could confide in him her true feelings towards Mr. Darcy, but that was a secret she dared not share, even with him. "I hope I shall like Pemberley."

"If you do not, I shall be most surprised. I only wish I were so fortunate as to have the opportunity to see it again myself some day."

His melancholy tone renewed her anger at Mr. Darcy, the cause of his exile. Without considering how it might betray her true allegiances, she said, "I would wish that for you as well."

An amiable smile graced his handsome features, and he stepped slightly closer to her. "You are most kind, Miss Bennet. Although Darcy and I have had our disagreements, I cannot fault his taste. How can I blame him for making the same choice I would have made had I his opportunities?"

Elizabeth looked down, conscious of the compliment in his words, yet feeling somehow disloyal for taking pleasure in it. Mr. Wickham must indeed sympathise with her position if he was willing to push the boundaries of propriety thus far to reassure her of his good will.

He must have known she dared not reply, since he added, "My only sorrow is that your fiancé is unlikely to permit any further acquaintance between us. In that way, your gain of Pemberley is my loss of a most pleasant companion."

"I hope that will not be the case, though it is unlikely our paths will cross after I leave Meryton."

"Who knows? Perhaps marriage will prove a moderating influence on Mr. Darcy. But I see Denny coming for me, so I will say my farewells now, in privacy." Holding her eyes with his own, he took her hand and kissed it, his lips lingering slightly longer than they should.

"Mr. Wickham," she murmured, uncomfortable with her awareness of him. She should not be enjoying his attentions. Before she could be entangled in a conversation with his fellow officers, she took her leave, her thoughts much in turmoil.

Chapter 4

ELIZABETH'S MEETING WITH MR. Wickham preoccupied her on the walk back to Longbourn. It was an unpleasant shock on her arrival to find Darcy waiting for her. Could he not leave her alone for even a few hours?

But as it happened, she had merely forgotten—or perhaps wished to forget—that her mother had invited him to dinner. So there was nothing to be done for it, although her lively spirits rebelled at the idea of spending her entire evening talking to him.

Lydia and Kitty seemed more determined than ever to embarrass Elizabeth with their antics. After her sisters had made several comments about the officers which left Elizabeth blushing for their sake, in desperation she asked Mr. Darcy to take a turn about the gardens with her, aware of the irony of seeking his company in such a way when her greatest desire was to have him far away. The sole advantage of marriage, she could see, was she would no longer have to concern herself with how her family humiliated her in front of Darcy.

She was not above using the situation to her own benefit, telling Darcy she had promised to make a last visit to her aunt Philips on the morrow, and she was sure he would be welcome if he cared to accompany her.

The look on his face spoke volumes. "I understand the necessity for saying farewell to your relations; however, I do not doubt I can find something to engage my interest at Netherfield while you do so."

Although it was the response she had hoped for, it still irritated her enough to cause her to react unwisely. With a sly glance, she said, "I saw several acquaintances in town today. Miss Lucas was on her way to the library, and I met Mr. Wickham outside the milliner's."

Darcy frowned. "You ought not associate with Mr. Wickham, Elizabeth. He is not the man he seems."

So Wickham had been correct in his assessment. "But we are acquaintances of some months' standing. I can scarcely escape it now." She took a perverse enjoyment in her assertion.

"You do not know the manner of man he is, and I hope you never will. Promise me you will not speak to him again."

Elizabeth had to look away from him, or she would have said something quite intemperate. It was of little consequence whether she promised or not; as she herself had said, it was unlikely their paths would cross again. Still, the taste was bitter in her mouth as she said, "Very well, if that is what you wish, sir."

The resolution did not prove as simple to keep as she had anticipated. When she arrived at her aunt's house, she discovered a small gathering in progress for the purpose of playing cards. Her aunt was seated at a table with several of the officers, their number including Mr. Wickham. Her pulse fluttered a little, wondering what he would think of her presence at such an occasion without her fiancé.

But she had made a promise. Elizabeth resolved that the best solution was to avoid Mr. Wickham, keeping to the side of the room away from the card players. Despite the initial success of this strategy, she did not move quickly enough when the game ended. Before she was aware what had transpired, she discovered Mr. Wickham taking the seat beside her. How was she to keep her word to Darcy now?

He smiled at her amiably. "Miss Elizabeth, you look quite lovely this evening."

Elizabeth met his eyes with a look intended to convey her apologies. After a minute of silence, Mr. Wickham said with concern, "Are you quite well?"

She bit her lip, willing him to understand. Her anger at Darcy for putting her in this position flared to life again.

It was unusual to catch Mr. Wickham with a frown on his face, but he wore one now. "Allow me to guess. You are forbidden to speak to me." His tone held anger and disbelief.

Elizabeth looked down at her hands, folded tightly in her lap.

"Of course. I do not know why I am surprised. This is hardly the first time he has taken from me something I valued on nothing more than a whim. But he cannot forbid *me* to speak to *you*." He paused, then continued in a low tone of restrained anger. "For your sake, I will not tarry. I would not wish to place you in jeopardy should someone report we were together. That you should be subject to such demands! If only I had the living I had been promised, I could have... But no matter. I would never have met you then. I have that, at least, to thank him for."

Elizabeth's lips turned into a slight smile, though her eyes were still downcast. Mr. Wickham was moving into the realm of outrageous flattery and flirtation, and owing to her prohibition on speech, she had no recourse to stop him. It was a fitting retribution for Mr. Darcy.

"I will ask only one thing of you before I go," he said. "When you are at Pemberley, when you walk along the edge of the stream and through the woods, will you remember me sometimes? It would be a comfort to know I should cross your mind from time to time. I know you cannot answer, so I must imagine your response and hope it is the one I wish for."

When he said no more, Elizabeth finally looked up at him again. He had apparently been waiting for that, since he leaned close to her and said in a low voice, "But I promised I would be brief, and I have already said too much. Remember me… Elizabeth." With a last caressing glance, he stood and left for the corner of the room where some of the younger people had collected for a dance.

Elizabeth watched him offer his hand to Lydia. She ought to be relieved he had left her side, since he had crossed the boundary into impudence. But she could not blame Wickham, given the provocation Darcy had given him by exacting her promise not to speak to him. She knew all too well where the true blame belonged.

❦

"I had thought Mr. Bingley might return to Netherfield for the wedding," Elizabeth said to Darcy the following day. It had been her dearest hope, perhaps her only hope, for the occasion: to have Jane and Bingley meet again.

"I thought it best not to suggest it to him."

Elizabeth wondered what that meant. "Is he aware of our wedding?"

"No, I plan to write to him once we reach Pemberley. He is often a visitor there, so it is likely you will see him soon enough."

But Jane would not. She could not imagine what excuse Darcy might manufacture for failing to invite his friend to their wedding. "It is of no matter. I was merely surprised."

Darcy turned to her and took her hand, a look of concern in his eyes. "Had you hoped for a larger wedding? Have I, in my haste to call you my own, deprived you of this?"

Somehow it was worse when he was kind. It would be easier in a way if he were always disagreeable. Why did he exempt *her* from his scorn for her family?

"No, not at all. I have no objection to the wedding plans." *Apart from their very existence*, she thought.

He did not seem reassured. "I hope you would tell me if something were not to your liking. I wish to make you happy, not to impose upon you."

It was too late for that. At least he meant well, even if his actions did not match his intention. Unfortunately, it did not begin to outweigh Elizabeth's anger over his interference with Mr. Bingley and Jane.

"I assure you, I am not in any way displeased," she said.

He looked at her with perplexity, as if she were a conundrum he could not make out.

Elizabeth was out of spirits the evening before her wedding. She did not know which would be worse, to deprive herself of this last night in the company of her family or to be forced to listen to their raptures about the morrow's events. Lydia and Kitty were delighted with their new gowns, and even Jane looked forward to the general society.

Mr. Darcy had elected not to join them for supper, preferring instead to remain at Netherfield with his sister. It was a relief to Elizabeth, who was having trouble enough maintaining a happy countenance on her last evening with her family. To her disappointment, her father had retired early to his library, unwilling to tolerate his wife's endless discourse on the finery that would be Elizabeth's once she was Mrs. Darcy.

Listening to her sisters speculate on which officers might attend the wedding, Elizabeth wondered when she would see her family again. Surely Mr. Darcy could not object if she travelled to Longbourn for a brief visit someday. Or perhaps he *would* object; she had been afraid to raise the question with him.

"You must go up to bed, Lizzy!" Mrs. Bennet cried, "You will need your sleep tomorrow." Elizabeth winced at her mother's coarseness and made her escape before it could become any worse.

Jane followed her up soon after, only to find her sister already in bed in the dark. She set the taper beside the mirror and began her nightly preparations as quietly as possible. But a sound, and then another, came from the direction of the bed.

She hurried over to sit beside Elizabeth, rubbing her shoulder with her hand. "Dearest Lizzy, you must not listen to our mother. I am certain tomorrow night will not be so bad. You will see."

Elizabeth had spent little thought on the prospect of her wedding night. It was just one more unpleasantness to come in a future that held little else. No matter how terrible the event might be, it would be nothing to spending her life with Mr. Darcy. She tried to still her sobs. "It is nothing, Jane. I am sad over leaving my home, no more. I will miss you so very much." The thought made her cry again.

Jane took her hand. "I know; but we will write often, will we not? I am looking forward to visiting you and seeing the famous Pemberley."

"I wish it could be so, but I must warn you, I do not believe I will be allowed to invite any of you to Pemberley." Elizabeth turned a tear-stained face to Jane. It was better to tell her now than to disappoint her hopes later on or, worse, make her think Elizabeth did not want her to visit.

"Not be allowed to! Lizzy, I cannot imagine what you are speaking of."

"Mr. Darcy does not approve of our family. The connection is a degradation to his pride. I cannot imagine he will welcome any of you to Pemberley."

"How could he not approve? He loves you. How could he fail to accept your family?" Jane asked soothingly.

"Jane, I know whereof I speak. He has often told me as much." Elizabeth buried her face in her pillow.

"I cannot believe it. You would not have chosen to marry such a man."

"I had no choice."

"Lizzy, what do you mean? Do not tell me he…" Jane paused, hesitating to think so ill of anyone, least of all her sister's husband-to-be.

"No, he did not hurt me. He kissed me where others could see. What else could I do but agree?"

"Oh, Lizzy, I am so sorry. But he is a good man; I am certain of it, and I know you will grow to care for him. It is obvious how much he loves you."

Elizabeth wiped her eyes, realising the distress she was causing to her most beloved sister, who had already paid a high enough price at Mr. Darcy's hand. "No doubt you are right, Jane. I am sure all will be well."

Chapter 5

ELIZABETH DID NOT LOOK back as the carriage pulled away from Longbourn, though her family was all outside to see the newlyweds on their way. Her lack of composure was such that she feared she might cry if she did, and she had already disgraced herself once before the wedding by bursting into tears in her father's arms outside the church door. Though everyone had commented kindly on her bridal nerves and her distress on leaving her family, Elizabeth did not doubt that Mr. Darcy must have been displeased when his bride appeared before him at the altar with red-rimmed eyes.

On the seat across from her, Mr. Darcy was watching her keenly. She shivered a little when she encountered his gaze. He said, "It has been an emotional day, has it not?"

She nodded, not trusting her voice. Something in her face must have alerted him, for he reached out to pull down the shade on the carriage window. Moving carefully across to her—even the luxurious Darcy carriage could not compensate for the uneven road—he sat down beside her and put his arm around her.

His unexpected kindness undermined her determination. Tears began to stream down her cheeks. With his free hand, he turned her face into his shoulder and held her while she wept.

When her sobs finally faded into exhausted despair, he cupped her face with his hand and dried her eyes tenderly with his handkerchief. "There, my love, it is not so bad, is it?" He leaned forward to kiss her gently.

He was being considerate and thoughtful, and the least she could do was to try to please him. She put her arms around his neck in the way he liked and let him kiss her. If she did not look forward to his kisses, at least they no longer troubled her; and it was comforting to have some human contact, even if it was with Mr. Darcy. Her husband. She wondered how long it would take her to become accustomed to that idea.

She was startled when Darcy's hand moved to cup her breast. No one had ever touched her there before, and the sensation was disturbing. She forced herself to imagine she was in London, in the busy sitting room of her uncle's house, while her aunt read poetry aloud. She could almost feel the heat of the fire burning on the hearth and hear the children at play. She concentrated on the picture she had created, and allowed her husband to do as he pleased.

Mr. Darcy took pains to remain at Elizabeth's disposal on her first full day at Pemberley. She was quieter than was her wont, and he feared she might be overwhelmed by her new home. Knowing her fondness for long walks, he showed her some of his favourite parts of the grounds; but although she admired them, he still suspected she was out of spirits. So he stayed near her constantly, holding her hand when he could and reassuring her of his devotion.

The following day, he had no choice but to spend at least a short while attending to business matters. He wished there were someone to whom he could entrust Elizabeth during the time, but she knew no one but him. Still, Elizabeth's strength of character had been one of her attractions for him, and he was certain that even if her sensibilities were still affected, she would be well enough until he returned. Even so, he couched his words with care. "I am sorry to leave you to your own devices so soon, Elizabeth, but I must meet my steward this afternoon to discuss what has happened in my absence. With luck, it will not take long, and I will be back by your side soon."

"Pray do not concern yourself on my behalf, sir. I am well able to entertain myself, and I would not wish to interfere with your business." An afternoon to herself sounded heavenly to Elizabeth.

"Is there anything I can arrange for your comfort? There is music for the pianoforte somewhere, and of course the library is at your complete disposal."

"Thank you, but I believe I will use the time to attend to my correspondence. I have several letters to write."

"To your family?"

"Yes, to let them know we are safely arrived. I am sure my mother is anxious to hear about Pemberley."

He frowned but said, "Very well."

"Is there a problem?" She could not deny he had been everything that was generous and gracious to her since their arrival, and she was resolved to do her best to meet his requirements in return.

"Not at all. It is considerate of you to inform them of our safe arrival, though afterwards, I see no reason to encourage your family to be overly familiar."

Was he saying what she thought he was? Did he wish her to have no contact with her family? With the caution now habitual in her interactions with him, she said, "Would you prefer, then, in general that I *not* write to my family?"

"I would prefer to minimise our connections with them."

He had never made a secret of his disdain for her family, but she was surprised even he would go to such an extent. Her anger rose. So he expected her to deny her family now she was his wife? She bit her tongue on a sharp retort, remembering Charlotte's words regarding the importance of not provoking her husband at this early stage, although as she spent time with him, she was beginning to doubt the possibility he might ever change his ways. Still, it would not hurt to be agreeable now and to think over her options at a calmer moment.

"Very well; I will take that under consideration." She hoped the words would not choke her.

He rose and came around the table to kiss her cheek. "Until later, then."

She did not know whether she was more shocked or furious, not only at his pride, but also at his unquestioning presumption she would agree with him in discarding her family. She had never argued with him when he disparaged them in the past, but could he actually believe her to be of the same mind? Did he think her so shallow that she would be willing to throw away her entire life for the chance to marry him? It was abominable. No wonder he had not wanted Bingley exposed to Jane again. If they had wed, it would be more difficult for Darcy to pretend his wife's family did not exist.

As the reality of it became evident, her spirits sank even lower. Now she truly would be dependent on him for everything.

＊

Even Elizabeth had to admit Darcy paid her every attention a new bride could wish for. He lavished her with gifts and walked with her through the park. On fine days, he often took her driving through the hills of Derbyshire. The wild landscape felt somehow alien to Elizabeth, but even so, she acknowledged its beauty. It was preferable to sitting alone, surrounded by the unwanted riches of Pemberley, thinking of what her life might have been.

He took her walking along the river at Dove Dale with scenery that could scarcely be matched. It was impossible not to take pleasure in it, and she said as much.

"If you enjoy this prospect, I can only assume you have a particular fondness for boulders." He took her hand in his.

"Fortunately, you have an abundance of them here in Derbyshire," she said with some of her old archness.

He looked pleased she thought. She must remember to praise the landscape more. She could not fault him for wanting her to like her new home.

Nor could she fault him for his behaviour towards her. He made a point of learning her tastes in books and bringing to her attention volumes in the library that might be of interest to her. Often he would ask her about them afterwards, much as her father had, although Darcy had the superior education. She generally found his points interesting. Although she did not always agree with them, she never said as much.

Once, when he was expressing a particularly strong opinion of a novel, she said, "Sir, if I did not know better, I would think you were trying to provoke me into an argument!"

"Perhaps I am." He sounded oddly wistful.

Despite his efforts, conversation between them often languished. Over time, she felt his intent gaze, which once she had thought critical, was turning more to one of puzzlement, as if he did not know quite what to make of her. Was he wondering why he had married her? She suspected he might have regrets given the objections to the match he had stated. She hoped he would not turn any disappointment on her, and she increased her efforts to be a proper wife.

His nightly visits showed no signs of flagging. She did not precisely dread them, once she was past her initial embarrassment at the act itself and the ways in which he touched her. He was invariably kind and gentle, and she was aware she had much to be thankful for in that regard. She had overheard enough stories about pain and humiliation in the marital bed to appreciate that. But it was difficult to feel gratitude when he was also the one who had placed her in this position.

She grew to almost enjoy the time afterwards when he made no further demands but held her in his arms. Her loneliness was such that it was comforting to be held, even by him, and to feel the warmth of his body against hers; and at those times she did not mind his kisses and caresses. They could be pleasant in a way, especially the touch of his hand as it moved along her body.

But that was later, and earlier in the visit, his touch could be troubling. He seemed to especially enjoy caressing those sensitive and secret parts of her which could create warm sensation in her. She fought against the feelings and schooled herself to lie still. If he knew her body responded to his touch in such an unladylike manner, it would be that much more proof of the inferiority and lack of respectability of her family. It was not for the mistress of Pemberley to find pleasure in the flesh.

He let her know clearly enough what pleased him. She discovered early on that he liked her to stroke his back underneath his nightshirt. This was simple enough. Other parts were more difficult. She felt relief each night when she heard the change in his breathing that indicated the end was near.

But Elizabeth was not formed for ill humour, and gradually, her natural spirits began to reassert themselves. Her maid bore greatest witness to this, as Elizabeth became more comfortable with her. Lucy was a lively girl herself, always ready with a touch of humour, and Elizabeth responded in kind. The other servants also saw something of Elizabeth's improved spirits, in particular the gardeners, who answered their new mistress's questions about the Pemberley grounds with quiet enthusiasm.

Elizabeth still experienced moments and even days of great loneliness, when she longed for the comfort of Jane's embrace or even her younger sisters' silliness. On occasion, the stark beauty of the Derbyshire landscape began to depress her, making her long for the green fields and quiet hills near Longbourn, but these days grew less frequent as time passed. The only person who remained without a hint of Elizabeth's gradual improvement was her husband, in whose company she still exercised the greatest of care. She was determined to give him no cause for complaint.

The situation continued until, one day, Darcy informed her he was expecting a brief visit from his cousin Colonel

Fitzwilliam en route to his new posting in the north. The excitement Elizabeth felt at this intelligence was more a reflection of her hunger for companionship than any particular interest in the colonel. If anything, she still felt a slight unease about him over the part he played in her engagement; and then, he himself had been quite attentive to her until Darcy's interest arose. Still, that was in the past, and she was quite indelibly married to Darcy now. She resolved to consider that history no more and instead to enjoy their guest's affability as best she could under the circumstances.

⁕

Elizabeth hummed as she prepared for bed. It was the most pleasant evening she could remember since coming to Derbyshire. Colonel Fitzwilliam's amiable company had been enjoyable, even more so since his presence seemed to bring out a new side of Darcy's personality, a laughing and lively side she quite appreciated after the sobriety to which she had grown accustomed. She hoped his mood would persist until he came to her that night—it would be easier for her to relax with him if he could be less serious. She might even be able to laugh with him.

She turned with a ready smile when he knocked at the adjoining door, but his countenance was grave, almost grim. Her smile faltered a little, but she greeted him pleasantly.

She could smell the brandy on his breath as he drew near her. He said no more than he had to and did no more than he needed to, skipping even the disquietingly pleasurable preliminaries. He was neither unkind nor rough, but she felt a discomfort she usually did not, and she could have wept from disappointment. When he was done, instead of holding her as was his custom, he left her bed. Elizabeth said impulsively, "Have I done something to displease you, sir?"

She regretted her words almost immediately when his face took on a sullen cast. "Displeased me?" he asked in a voice laden with cynicism. "No, madam, you are always as careful not to displease me as you seem careful not to *please* me."

Elizabeth paled. "I do not know what makes you think that. I try to please you."

"Then why does it require my cousin's presence to show me the woman I thought I was marrying is not dead? Why is it you can laugh with *him* and tease *him*? Was I a second-best for you, since he could not afford you? Or was marrying me simply an expedient way to stay in contact with him?" His words came out with bitter alacrity, as if they had been running through his mind for some time.

Stunned, Elizabeth said in angry disbelief, "Surely you cannot believe that I…" She stopped herself, then continued in a more reasonable voice, "It is true I was glad to see him, but not at all for the reasons you seem to think. I should have been at least as glad to see many other people of my acquaintance—Mrs. Collins, Mr. Bingley, my sister Jane. I have not yet made friends in Derbyshire, and I miss my past acquaintances."

"Your argument would be more persuasive, madam, if you ever showed any of the same warmth towards me," he said, his voice cold as he advanced towards her.

Her heart pounded in a mixture of resentment and fear. Her husband was clearly half in his cups, he was angry at her, and she was quite alone with him, in nothing but her nightdress, his seed still wet between her legs. She was completely at the mercy of the man who had ruined Wickham's life on a whim. Closing her eyes, she turned her face away into the pillow. If he was going to strike her, she did not wish to see it coming.

But no blow came. Instead, she heard only the harshness of his breathing. "You have no response, I see."

Elizabeth bit her lip. "I do not know what response you wish me to make."

"An honest one, by God! Was he the one you wanted?"

"I never wanted him. I barely know him." Her voice was low but firm.

"Then why have you changed so, ever since our engagement? Why did you agree to marry me? Was it for my possessions?"

She shook her head dumbly.

He sat on the edge of the bed and grasped her shoulders. "Answer my question, Elizabeth!"

It could no longer be avoided. "Because you compromised me." She spoke barely above a whisper, as if by remaining quiet she could avoid his rage.

"Because I *what?*" He dropped his hands away from her, looking at her with disbelief.

"You kissed me, and we were observed." Her voice was a little stronger this time as she claimed her truth.

"You had already accepted me!"

"I had done no such thing. You declared yourself, but I said nothing, not a word."

His eyes narrowed. "You are splitting hairs. You would have accepted me in any case."

Elizabeth wished she could throw the truth in the face of his arrogance, but a wiser part of her prevailed, and she said nothing.

Darcy swung to his feet and paced across the room. "So you would like to believe you would have refused me. On what grounds?" He wore the haughty look she remembered so well from Hertfordshire.

She felt too vulnerable, lying in bed looking up at his tall form, so she pushed herself to a sitting position, resting her back against the headboard. "You ruined my beloved sister's happiness. You disparaged my family. You had given offence to almost everyone of my acquaintance, and Mr. Wickham himself told me how you had misused him."

"Mr. Wickham!" he said contemptuously. "What lies has he told you?"

"He told me how you disregarded your father's will!" Now she had begun, it was impossible to stop the words from tumbling out. "My feelings have only been confirmed by your attitude towards my family. My aunt Gardiner is in every way the superior of Lady Catherine—in manners, in education, in behaviour—yet you treat her as less than nothing. I do not deny my mother's lack of seemliness, but even she would not lock away and attempt to dominate her child's every movement and thought as your aunt does. My sister Jane, whom you thought not good enough for your friend, has never uttered an unkind word in her life, yet you disdain her. It is intolerable."

Darcy stared at her in savage disbelief. Surely she could not mean what she was saying? Could she have deceived him since their very first day together? He could see the accusation in her eyes. Every inch of him screamed to deny it, but the truth was there before him. It was not that she liked his cousin better, but that she hated him. What a self-deluded fool he had been! He said in an icy tone, "I can see I am quite unwelcome here. I bid you good night, madam." Fearing his ability to control himself, he stalked out of her room and closed the adjoining door behind him, the same door whose existence had given him such ineffable pleasure when he first brought Elizabeth to Pemberley.

He retreated into the darkness of his bedchamber. The jealousy he had felt earlier seemed trivial now.

Elizabeth did not love him. She had never loved him. She had taken him to her bed, again and again, with nothing but dislike and contempt in her heart.

He did not know how he was to live through the night.

Chapter 6

ELIZABETH'S EYES BARELY CLOSED during the night. The scene with Darcy kept replaying itself before her eyes. What had possessed her to utter such words to the man who held complete control over her life? Had it not been difficult enough without earning her husband's enmity? If she had felt alone before, it was nothing to what she would experience now, without even his conversation for company. She had no resources, nowhere to turn for support, no matter how unkind he became. She was his wife and, in the eyes of the law, his property. He could do whatever he liked to her, and she would have no recourse. It was precisely the situation she had always feared and why she had wished to marry for affection.

When dawn lit the windows, she knew choices must be made. One obvious course was to avoid aggravating Darcy's jealousy of Colonel Fitzwilliam. She did not go down to breakfast, and she managed to find enough small tasks to prevent her from making anything more than the briefest of greetings to their guest during the day. She could not evade him at dinner, but she chose to speak only when spoken to, playing an old game of pretending to be Jane and answering each question as Jane would. She suppressed her instinct to avoid meeting her husband's eyes and, instead, acted as if nothing unusual had passed between them. *His* coolness, however, was unmistakable.

He did not appear in her bedchamber that night. Elizabeth, sick with relief at the respite, wondered how long it would continue. Though his displeasure with her was clear, neither his words nor actions were reproachable. It occurred to Elizabeth he might be biding his time until Colonel Fitzwilliam left, not wishing to act out his marital discord in front of his cousin. The day she stood at Darcy's side, waving good-bye to the Colonel in his carriage, she felt true panic.

But nothing changed. Darcy avoided looking at her and spoke to her only as necessary and to preserve appearances in front of the servants. Nor did he come to her room or seek out her company at any point. However little she might return his affection, she had grown to enjoy his companionship, at least compared to the barrenness of the remainder of her life. She wondered how long his silence would last and if it would ever end. But even she, who once had not hesitated to speak her mind to the formidable Lady Catherine de Bourgh, now found she dared not approach her grimly silent husband.

She dreaded their meals together. It was difficult to eat when faced with his hostility, and she had little appetite in any case. Still, she forced herself to appear for meals and nodded in agreement with anything he said.

One morning at breakfast, he gave her a perfunctory greeting but, as was now his custom, said nothing until the servants came in to clear the dishes. Then he said, "Your aunt and uncle Gardiner are making a northern tour soon, are they not?"

She was startled to hear him raise the subject of her family. "Yes, I believe that is still their plan."

"Where do they intend to travel?"

"The last I heard they hoped to go to the Lakes." And would God she were still unmarried and going with them as originally planned! She swallowed a lump in her throat.

"They are likely to travel through Derbyshire, then," he said, his voice as remote as ever. "You should invite them to stay here on their way."

Elizabeth raised her eyes to stare at him. She could hardly question him with the servants listening to every word. It was hard to credit he was changing his position on her family when his voice and countenance were devoid of warmth.

Whether he meant her to act on it or not, surely it was an olive branch, and she did not want him to think her ungrateful. "Thank you. It is very generous of you."

"I shall see you at dinner, then, madam," he said, clearly intending an end to the conversation, and he took his departure.

Afterwards, she puzzled over his behaviour. She could not imagine he would actually wish any of her family to be at Pemberley, even if he were willing to suffer it for her sake. Perhaps he was tired of the coldness between them and intended this as a gesture of his willingness to compromise. Yes, most likely that was it.

If so, she would meet him halfway; she did not wish to spend the rest of her life like this. She considered what she could do in return, but she had nothing to offer him. Finally, the memory of his words during their quarrel returned: *"What lies has Mr. Wickham told you?"* Perhaps she could respond to that, show a willingness to hear his side of the story. After all, it was not as if Wickham had offered her any proof of his tale, and perhaps it was open to more than one interpretation. She had to admit that Wickham's description of Darcy's behaviour was not consistent with what she herself had observed in him; he was a generous and fair landlord, and it was hard to imagine him deliberately cheating someone.

It was even possible, she supposed, that what Darcy had suggested was true: that Wickham had lied to her. A sensation of coldness came over her at the thought; what if she had believed the wrong man and levelled false accusations at her husband? Wickham had never given her any cause to disbelieve him, but she should have sought out the truth of the matter long ago.

It took her until afternoon to convince herself to act on the question. She went to Darcy's study and hesitated at the closed door, shutting her eyes as if trying to summon her courage. Delaying would do her no good. She knocked firmly at the door. On hearing her husband's voice, she entered.

She advanced until she stood several feet from his desk and folded her hands in front of her. His eyes flickered up at her, then looked down again to the papers in front of him. He dipped his pen in the inkwell, blotted it, and began to write. "Yes, madam?"

He had not called her by name, nor even Mrs. Darcy, since their quarrel. She moistened her lips with the tip of her tongue. "It has occurred to me, sir, that there are often two sides to a story. In the matter of Mr. Wickham, I have heard only *his* side."

He did not look up. "I cannot argue that point."

Clearly he did not intend to make this easy for her. She told herself it should be no surprise; he himself had said he was of a resentful temper, and she had without doubt lost his good opinion. Very well, he would see she was no coward. She lifted her chin. "I wondered if perhaps you would care to tell me your side of the story."

His pen stilled, and after a moment, he replaced it in its stand. Leaning down, he opened a drawer and sorted through it until he removed a document. He looked at it for a moment then held it out to her. "I will not trouble you with explanations you are unlikely to believe," he said, "but this, I hope, should be enough to acquit me of cruelty towards Mr. Wickham."

She took the paper from his hand and examined it. It was a receipt, signed by George Wickham and dated some five years previously, for three thousand pounds in return for which he quitted all claim to the living at Kympton as promised him in the will of Mr. Darcy. She continued to look at it for some moments after she had already perused it. Finally, with a dry mouth, she said, "It seems I believed the wrong man. You have my most sincere apologies, sir."

"You are not the first woman he has worked his wiles upon, nor, I daresay, will you be the last," he said brusquely, taking back the document. "Is there anything else, madam?"

She was being dismissed. "No, nothing else." She should thank him for answering her question, but she could not bring herself to say the words. Instead, she turned and left the room, not stopping until she reached the front door and found her way out into the woods of Pemberley. Heedless of her delicate indoor slippers, she struck off along a path which would take her out of sight of the house as quickly as possible.

She had her answer now. She had believed a man for no better reason than that he had flattered her and disbelieved the man who had fallen in love with her and married her and, whatever his other faults, had never attempted to disguise the truth. Now she had earned his implacable resentment, and there was nothing to be done for it. She had never wanted his love, but his hatred was worse, especially as they were destined to live together regardless of their wishes.

She could not but blame herself for her gullibility and her willingness to believe Mr. Wickham's lies as well as for her own anger, which had caused her to fling such intemperate accusations at her husband. She did not hold him faultless; he should never have said what he did to her about his cousin, and he continued his aggravating habit of assuming she would believe whatever he wished her to believe. However, she could not deny she had hurt, deeply hurt, a man who loved her enough to marry her over many objections and had never treated her with anything but kindness—apart from the matter of her family. If she had been cheated of having a marriage based on love, he had been cheated yet further. But he had refused her peace offering; all that remained was for her to treat him as befitted a man who had been kind and generous to her.

It was near dinnertime, and she set out towards the house again. She had gone only a short way before realising she had taken a wrong turning. Attempts to retrace her steps proved fruitless, and with a sigh of exasperation, she set off towards higher ground from which she might be able to see the house and re-establish her direction.

Her strategy was successful, although not immediately; she eventually made her way back to Pemberley House, but it was near dark when she arrived, and she was somewhat the worse for wear owing to leaving the paths to follow a more direct route. She was greeted at the door by the butler, who exclaimed, "Mrs. Darcy!"

She was weary, and she did not feel her appearance warranted such a degree of startlement. Her voice was a trifle sharp as she said, "If you would be so kind as to arrange for my supper to be sent up to my room, I would appreciate it." She went past him into the hallway.

"Madam, please, I believe the master wishes to see you."

"Please tell him that I will wait on him as soon as I have taken a moment to refresh myself." She would prefer not to appear before him in tattered slippers and a dirty petticoat.

Her wishes were destined to be thwarted, as Darcy appeared in the hall before she could quit it. "Elizabeth! Where have you been?"

She had to rein in irritation at his tone. She stood very still to hide her torn slippers beneath her skirts. "I was walking in the park and lost my way. It took me a little time to get my bearings. My apologies if you were concerned."

"Concerned!" he exclaimed angrily. "My steward has been organizing men to search for you!"

"Surely you knew I would find my way back," she said in an attempt to be reasonable.

"In the dark or if there were... an accident?"

"You have my apologies, sir. What further would you like?"

"I would like..." He paused, apparently struggling for self-control. "I would like you to be more careful, at least until you know the park better."

She inclined her head in agreement, thinking it best to say nothing. At least he had not forbidden her to walk out altogether, even though it had obviously cost him something not to do so. "If you will excuse me, then?"

"As you wish," he said. For a moment, Elizabeth thought she saw the flicker of his old look in his eyes, but then it was gone again and replaced by implacability.

She thought about that look again as she sat in her bed in her nightdress, her arms wrapped around her knees. Did it mean that some small morsel of love remained within him? Perhaps so, but if it did, it seemed he regretted it. She found the idea oddly painful.

She could not continue in this manner. She needed to decide her best course of action regarding her marriage. The simplest answer was to go on as she had been, polite and compliant, but perhaps now with the addition of avoiding him as much as possible, since he no longer had any desire for her company. That would be dutiful, and no one could hold it against her. The harder option would be to try to give him what he claimed to want—the laughing, smiles, and teasing she had shown Colonel Fitzwilliam. She did not know whether it was within her capability, at least when he was as forbidding as he was now. She had done it before their engagement though, despite the fact that she disliked him; why should being married to him make it so much more difficult?

The worst of it was at night, like this, when she lay awake wondering if he intended to come to her. He had not been to her bedchamber since their quarrel, but that would change sooner or later, she had no doubt, and she was frightened of it. It had been difficult enough accustoming herself to the liberties he took with her body when he had been kind and gentle. She shuddered to think what it would be like if he came to her in anger.

Unbeknownst to Elizabeth, Darcy sat in his study until the rest of the household was abed, turning a pair of torn slippers flecked with blood in his hands. What had he done to her? Marriage to a man she disliked. He wondered what she had thought when he kissed her, when he was in her bed. Was it repulsion or merely distaste? He told himself, as he had many times in the past few days, not to think on it, but he was as unsuccessful as he had been every other time.

How could he keep from blaming himself? He had taken the woman he loved as if she were a toy he wanted and had killed the spirit which he loved her for. Now he was fated to spend the rest of his life facing a simulacrum of Elizabeth, remembering what she had been and the joy he had felt so briefly when he believed she cared for him. It was a fitting punishment for his selfishness that he should lose what he valued most. But she did not deserve to suffer.

How had he, with all the advantages of his birth and intellect, come to the point where he could think of no better outcome than that he might die young? At least then Elizabeth might have a chance at happiness. He ran his fingers over the dark stains on her slippers. Perhaps it was too late even for that.

Chapter 7

AT BREAKFAST MR. DARCY said, "Have you written to your aunt and uncle yet, madam?"

Elizabeth carefully broke her toast in two parts. "No, sir, I have not."

"Why have you not?"

"I wished to avoid embarrassment. I believe they plan to visit nearby, in Lambton, and I shall call on them there." Seeing his frown, she added, "You need not fear; my aunt and uncle are people of the world and understand the situation. They will not claim a relationship with you." Did he have any idea how much it cost her to speak of this as if it were of no matter? She turned her attention to buttering her toast as if the outcome of the Peninsular War depended on her thoroughness.

"Elizabeth, that was not my meaning."

She did not raise her eyes. "I would not wish to make you uncomfortable in any way, sir."

"Instead you insist on making *yourself* uncomfortable, as if that would be without effect on me. I was wrong to criticise your family. They are welcome here."

She was uncertain what to make of this unprecedented admission. His tone spoke more of irritation than of kindness. "I... thank you."

"Have I ever given you cause to be frightened of me?" he asked brusquely.

His words had the effect of forcing her to meet his eyes, and what she saw there was different from the message his voice gave her. "No. You have always been very kind to me." It was true; her fears were more of what he *might* do if he chose than of anything he had done. Recalling her resolve, she gave him a playful look. "Apart from a few moments when you rode that stallion of yours."

"You mean Hurricane? He is not as bad as his name suggests. But you never ride, do you?"

"No, I have always preferred walking. When I was young, I saw a man fall from horseback, and I never cared to learn after that."

"If I found you a very gentle mare, would you consider trying it?"

"If you like, sir," she said, though in truth she would prefer not to.

"No, if you like," he said sharply. "I am not trying to force it on you. It is merely that Derbyshire has many sights I believe you would enjoy that are inaccessible by carriage and too far to walk. I should not like to see you deprived of them."

She considered this for a minute. "Could it be a very *small* mare?" she asked doubtfully.

He smiled slightly, as if to himself. "The smallest and gentlest I can find."

"Well, then, I shall *try*. I do not promise to continue."

He raised an eyebrow. "That is all I can ask."

She had to admit he seemed happier when she challenged him than when she offered immediate compliance. If he wanted her as she had been in Hertfordshire and at Rosings, he must like some challenge. At least their discourse ended in a civil tone this time. Surely that must be progress.

<hr/>

Elizabeth noticed a small box sitting among her toiletries when she sat before her mirror the next morning to brush out her hair. Puzzled, she opened it to reveal a delicate gold pendant on a chain. She frowned; there was only one person it could be from, and she was not expecting gifts from him. He had always given her presents in person in the past, and she did not deserve anything now. Was it another gesture of peace? Or perhaps it was something he had bought for her long since for some future occasion and now wanted to rid himself of—that would explain the indirect presentation, she supposed. She touched it lightly, feeling the cold hardness of it beneath her fingers.

She wore it down to breakfast, only to discover Darcy had already eaten and was out riding. It bought her a little time, but it made her wonder if he did not want to discuss it with her. Still, if he was making an attempt to mend the breach between them, she wanted him to know she appreciated it.

When he returned to the house, she sought him out in his study. Unlike his actions of a few days earlier, he rose politely when she came in and gestured her to a chair. She shook her head, but in a friendly manner. "Thank you for the necklace, sir. It is lovely."

"There is no need for thanks; the pleasure will be mine in seeing you wear it," he said formally.

"Well, you have my thanks anyway, and you may do with them what you will." On an impulse, she stepped around his desk and bent to kiss him lightly on the cheek.

He did not look pleased at her initiative. She backed away hastily, saying, "I shall see you at dinner, then, Mr. Darcy."

"I want no more duty kisses, Elizabeth. Their taste is bitter."

Stung, she replied, "That was not out of duty, unless you would have it so, but I will keep your chastisement in mind." She hastened away to her room, feeling unequal to meeting anyone.

So a reconciliation was not his desire. She removed the necklace and threw it on the table, not wanting it against her skin any longer. She should have listened to her first instinct and said nothing. Had he wanted thanks, he would have given it to her himself.

She did not wish to take the risk of encountering her husband again, so she spent much of the afternoon curled up in the window seat with a book. The novel could not hold her interest. She was angry he had spoken to her in such a way and both hurt and disappointed he had rejected her overture. If her efforts of the past few days were for naught, what was she to do next? She wished desperately for Jane or even Charlotte to confide in; they had always understood Darcy better than she did and would believe she meant well. But there was nothing for it but to make her own decisions. For now, she would follow his lead whenever they met.

There was no point in attempting to avoid him at dinner; she would only be delaying facing him till breakfast. She chose a different necklace when she dressed for dinner, selecting for her own comfort a topaz cross she had owned as Elizabeth Bennet.

He was waiting for her outside the dining room when she came down. Unsmilingly, he escorted her to her chair but paused once she was seated. She looked up at him, and he laid his fingers lightly on the side of her neck. "I prefer the other necklace," he said.

"I do not like duty gifts." She was uncomfortably aware this was the first time since their quarrel he had touched her. The warmth of his fingers against her skin felt almost shocking.

"I ought not to have said that earlier; I have regretted it," he said with a straight, serious look. "I would not wish you to feel you cannot approach me. I hope you will wear the necklace again. It was not given out of duty."

"Why else?" she said, the hurt which had been brewing in her all afternoon coming to the surface. "I know I am a disappointment to you; you need not pretend otherwise."

He took his seat at the head of the table. "I will not attempt to disguise that our circumstances are not what I had hoped for, but it is not you who disappoints me."

"It is kind of you to say so," she said uncomfortably, not knowing how to respond to a statement so patently untrue.

"I took the liberty of writing to your aunt and uncle to extend the invitation for them to visit us here."

"You did?" exclaimed Elizabeth, startled. Recovering herself, she said, with what she hoped would be a teasing inflection, "I hope you will not regret it, sir. At least they are travelling without their children. My cousins might be more than even the most patient of men could bear."

"They seemed well behaved enough when I met them in London."

"If so, it was no doubt a chance occurrence, a temporary whim of the moment on their part."

He seemed to realise he was being teased and smiled slightly. "However you would have it, madam, they are invited."

"Yes, I see that when your mind is made up to a matter, there is no arguing with you." She returned his smile a little shyly.

"While we are on the subject of my stubbornness, Elizabeth, I should mention I have found a horse for you. Perhaps you would permit me to introduce you to her in the morning." There was a challenge in his voice.

"I would be happy to be *introduced*," she said, staking her own ground in the matter.

He seemed willing to accept this and turned the conversation to household matters, as if there were no difficulties between them at all. Elizabeth was willing to maintain this pretence as well, out of sheer relief for the cessation of hostilities. She only hoped it would last.

The horse was a lovely chestnut, small as he had promised, but with elegant lines. Elizabeth reached out to pat her neck, and the mare whickered softly, turning large dark eyes on her. "Hello, pretty girl," Elizabeth said, stroking her.

"She arrived yesterday, but I wanted her to settle in before you met her," said Darcy. "I have it on good authority she is very gentle and docile."

"No doubt more docile than I! She is lovely. Thank you."

"The pleasure is mine." He looked at her quizzically. "I admit I am confused. I was under the impression you disliked horses."

"Oh, no. I like horses. It is only *riding* them I do not like."

"Perhaps that may yet change."

She arched an eyebrow at him. "Perhaps. Does she have a name?"

"Her previous owner called her Pandora. You can change it if you like." If Darcy was attempting to hide his smile, he was not succeeding.

She laughed. "No, I think Pandora is perfect. Is it not?" Her eyes sparkled as she looked at him.

"For her or for you?"

"I hope I am not opening Pandora's box by agreeing to this," she said.

"We shall see." Darcy led the mare to the mounting block then turned to look at Elizabeth, silently challenging her.

She walked over to the block and paused, gazing at it as if it were a mountain to be climbed. With a sigh, she stepped up, reminding herself the ground in the enclosure was free of rocks and she would not be high up; but she did not move quickly. If this was what it took to improve her husband's opinion of her, she would do it. She closed her eyes for a moment, then gingerly seated herself on the sidesaddle, holding tightly onto the pommel.

"Very good," Darcy said. "If you straighten your back, I think you will find it more comfortable."

"When did you become an expert at riding sidesaddle, sir?" Impertinence helped disguise her fear.

"One can learn a great deal by observation."

Elizabeth's hands gripped the saddle as he slapped the mare lightly with the reins. She would let him lead her once around the stable yard, no more, and then she would stop she decided.

She was surprised that Darcy himself was taking on this task. She had expected to be relegated to a stable hand for this stage of her lessons. But perhaps he thought she would not try it if he were not there.

Pandora's gaits were reassuringly smooth, but Elizabeth's heart pounded at each step. They were a quarter of the way around, then halfway, then almost back to the mounting block.

"That is enough, I believe," she said, her voice scarcely obeying her. "I would like to stop now."

Darcy did not argue, leading her directly back to the block. He turned to her to offer his hand, looking taken aback at the sight of her face.

"I am sorry, Elizabeth; I should not have asked you to try this. I do not wish for you to make yourself uncomfortable." The concern in his voice was evident.

Gratefully she stepped onto the block. "You did not force me," she said.

"No, but I asked it of you. It did not occur to me that a woman who dared stand up to Lady Catherine could possibly find riding alarming. It was my mistake. I will have her put away now."

"No," said Elizabeth, her voice a little stronger, "I think I will go around one more time first."

"Are you certain?" He did not sound convinced.

"Yes." She settled herself back in the saddle.

It was not quite so bad the second time, but she was relieved to dismount. This time Darcy said nothing beyond calling for a stable boy to take the horse.

That night at dinner Darcy asked how she was recovering from the morning's exercise.

"Well enough, sir," she replied.

"I apologise that it caused you distress."

"You must think me very foolish to be so frightened of riding." She was curious to see how he would handle this challenge, but she also wished to continue the conversation. Her riding was one of the very few subjects they could discuss without conflict.

"Not foolish. I do not understand why you would feel that way, but many people have irrational fears. I do not doubt your courage."

"But I cannot believe *you* would ever be subject to irrational fears." *Or if he were, he would never admit to them*, she thought.

"I would not say that." He appeared completely preoccupied with cutting his meat.

"I cannot imagine what irrational fears you might possess."

He took a bite and chewed it slowly before answering. "I fear losing the people I care for."

"That is hardly irrational. Who would not fear that?"

"True, but I perhaps worry about it disproportionately. I also dislike heights, though I have learned to overcome it to a large degree."

It made him a little more human somehow, yet Elizabeth wondered about the disproportionate worry he was so reluctant to speak of. And yet, he had spoken of it, when he quite easily could have denied any fears. Apparently, he could still surprise her.

"I believe tomorrow I will try again with Pandora and see if I have learned anything," she said.

An expression she could not interpret crossed Darcy's face, then was quickly hidden.

"If you will inform me when you intend to do so, I will accompany you," Darcy said.

"There is no need to interrupt you. One of the stable hands can assist me." She did not wish to be any trouble to him, especially when they were just establishing amicable relations.

"I would prefer to be there, unless you object."

"I will be certain to inform you then." She wondered why he wanted to be there. If he merely wanted to know if she followed her plan, all he would have to do was to ask a servant. But perhaps he, too, recognised the importance of having an activity they could share safely. She hoped so; it would mean he had not yet completely given up on her.

Chapter 8

THE NEXT MORNING, DARCY led Elizabeth around the stable yard again. It was no easier for having done it the previous day, but this time she managed to make the circuit of the stable yard twice before asking to stop. She was equally proud of her success in achieving another period of civility with her husband.

She spent the remainder of the morning writing a letter to Jane. It was not a letter she expected to send. She did not yet feel comfortable resuming the correspondence without Darcy's express direction, though she expected this new polite Darcy would not object if she asked. Still, she did not wish to risk their tentative reconciliation. But writing the letter helped clarify some of her thoughts and strengthened her determination to ease the disquietude in her marriage. That would be Jane's advice.

She was interrupted by a footman. "Miss Darcy has arrived, madam," he said.

"Miss Darcy?" Elizabeth had heard the sound of a carriage a few minutes earlier but had thought little of it, as no guests were expected, certainly not Miss Darcy. At least not that Mr. Darcy had mentioned. Perhaps he was well aware of this plan. Hurriedly, Elizabeth smoothed her skirts and descended to the main sitting room.

Georgiana was in her brother's embrace, her head against his shoulder. "I told them you had sent for me. They were..." Her words trailed off as she noticed Elizabeth's presence and extricated herself from her brother's arms.

"Do not give it another thought." Darcy's voice was tender, as once it had been when he spoke to Elizabeth.

It felt presumptuous for Elizabeth to welcome Georgiana to her own home, yet under these circumstances she needed to say something. She advanced towards the younger girl and kissed her cheek. "How lovely to see you again, Georgiana."

Georgiana gave a proper curtsey. "Thank you." Her voice was colourless.

"How was your journey?"

Georgiana glanced at her brother before answering. "It went well, thank you."

Elizabeth felt very much *de trop*. "You must have a great deal to tell one another. I shall look forward to seeing you at dinner." She retreated, making her way quickly to her rooms, where she settled herself in her favourite chair and picked up her embroidery, hoping, rather than believing, it would be enough to distract her from her thoughts.

Choosing a length of azure thread, she prepared her needle. Why had Darcy not told her he had sent for Georgiana? Surely he could not have thought Elizabeth would object; she had not objected to anything since their marriage. Perhaps he had not wished to explain his plans to her. The most likely reason he would send for his sister was all too obvious: he must desire some companionship more congenial to him than her own. Knotting the thread, she stabbed the needle through the delicate fabric.

It would make no difference to her own situation, since she saw him only at meals and at her brief riding lessons. So why did it trouble her so?

She waited to see if Darcy would seek her out with an explanation or at least some information on the length of Georgiana's visit, but he did not appear by the time she had finished embroidering the flowers around her new initials. Elizabeth Darcy. Pemberley may be her home officially, but she was its mistress in name only.

She felt a surge of loneliness. Somewhere Georgiana and Darcy were no doubt enjoying one another's company. Running her finger over the embroidered "E.D.," Elizabeth wondered if Darcy would continue his recent kindness to her now that he had Georgiana for companionship or if she would be just another body inhabiting the lovely, echoing house.

Unable to tolerate being imprisoned indoors any longer, she put her work aside. After a quick stop in the kitchens, she made her way to the stables to seek out the only company which might truly be pleased to see her.

Pandora whickered softly and swished her tail when she saw Elizabeth. "No ride this afternoon, girl, just a treat." She held out a lump of sugar. The horse's warm breath moved over her palm as she ate. "I have a carrot for you, too." Breaking the carrot into pieces as she had seen the manservant at Longbourn do, she offered them one at a time. At least she could make someone happy.

Elizabeth stayed a few minutes in Pandora's stall, talking nonsense and patting her neck. She would have liked to stay longer, but the stable boys would have wondered at that. Slowly, she trudged past the long line of stalls. It was a far cry from the corner of the barn that held Longbourn's two horses. Her mind thus occupied, she was startled to hear her name spoken when she stepped out into the watery grey daylight.

It was Georgiana, dressed in an elegant riding habit which accentuated her height and womanly figure. Behind her, a groom held a finely boned horse, nervous looking and easily two hands taller than Pandora.

"Georgiana! I had thought you would be resting after your travels." Elizabeth tried to ignore how the horse threw his head and stamped his feet impatiently.

"I miss my horses so much when I am away. I can never wait to go riding when I come home."

"I hope you have a lovely time." Elizabeth could not imagine ever wanting to ride such a horse.

Georgiana cast her eyes down Elizabeth's dress, obviously unsuited for riding then glanced into the stables. "What brings you here?"

Elizabeth smiled ruefully. "I was visiting my horse. She is new, and I try to stop by when I can so she will become accustomed to me."

"You have a new horse?" For the first time in their brief acquaintance, Georgiana sounded truly interested in what Elizabeth had to say.

"Your brother gave her to me." She did not know why she felt as if she should apologise for having a new horse.

"May I see her?"

"Of course." Elizabeth did not understand Georgiana's excitement, but if this might prove a way for the girl to be more comfortable with her, she would try it. She led the way back to the stall. "This is Pandora." The little mare's ears flickered, clearly surprised to see Elizabeth again so soon, and she pushed her head against Elizabeth's shoulder, as if hoping for another treat.

Georgiana's expression was blank. "*This* is your horse?"

Elizabeth almost winced at the disbelief in her voice. Small, sedate Pandora was nothing like Georgiana's horse. Elizabeth moved a little closer to Pandora, remembering what Wickham had said of Georgiana's pride. "Yes, she is."

"She is lovely," Georgiana said a moment too late. "Who are her sire and dam?"

"I do not believe your brother mentioned that to me. But I ought not keep you from your ride." Elizabeth stepped outside the stall. This humiliating conversation could not end soon enough.

Georgiana suddenly looked awkward. "Yes, of course. If you will excuse me." She hurried out of the stable.

Elizabeth followed more slowly, emerging just in time to see Georgiana mount and trot out of the stable yard then urge her horse to a canter. She cut as fine a figure on horseback as her brother did. Elizabeth watched as she raced towards a fence and closed her eyes involuntarily as the horse leapt into the air.

After dinner the following day, Darcy asked Georgiana to play for them. Elizabeth was unsurprised by the agility with which Georgiana's hands moved over the keys. She had already learned how far the quiet girl's education outstripped her own haphazard one. When the music ended, Elizabeth smiled and applauded, joining her praises to Darcy's.

As Georgiana began a second piece, Darcy turned to Elizabeth. "You did not ride this morning."

"No, I did not." Elizabeth had not felt inclined to display her own lack of ability after Georgiana's show of horsemanship. She had been glad of her decision that afternoon when she had seen Georgiana and Darcy cantering across the hills and later listened through the open door to their happy conversation when they finally returned from their ride.

Darcy appeared to choose his words with care. "Is there anything I can do to make riding more pleasant for you?"

"I cannot think of anything, thank you." She was uncomfortably aware this was their first even partially private conversation since Georgiana's arrival.

"If you should feel inclined to try again another day, I would be happy to assist."

"There is little point."

"As you wish." Darcy lapsed into silence as Georgiana's music continued to flow past.

Elizabeth felt unaccountably near tears. She did not know what she wished he might say; she would likely have resented it had he pressed her further. She wondered if he would sell Pandora now, rather than bear the cost of keeping a mount best suited to a child.

His voice interrupted her thoughts. "If I have done something to offend you, I hope you will tell me, as I appear to be singularly incapable of divining it by myself."

She turned to look at him in surprise. "No, I am not offended." How could she be offended that he loved his sister or that Georgiana rode and played better than she ever would? "But I would appreciate if the next time you are expecting company, I might be informed in advance."

"Ah." Darcy's brow cleared. "If you are referring to Georgiana, I had no notion she was coming. I would certainly have told you otherwise."

Elizabeth was more relieved than she wanted to admit. "I thought I heard her say you had sent for her."

Darcy glanced at the pianoforte, a grim look settling around his mouth. "There were some difficulties with my aunt. Georgiana is painfully frightened of conflict and wished to leave. She told my uncle I had sent for her."

"I find it hard to believe she would ever feel intimidated."

"Georgiana? She is frightened of almost everything except horses and her music, and that is only because she practises constantly and has ridden almost since she could walk."

Elizabeth blinked in surprise. If he was correct, and presumably he was, then she had misunderstood Georgiana as much as she had misread him initially. Still, she could not shake the image of him laughing with his sister as their horses had hurtled along the landscape. "She is an excellent horsewoman. Even if I rode every day for the rest of my life, I would never ride like that."

"I am happy to hear that. Georgiana can be somewhat reckless on horseback."

A few minutes earlier, Elizabeth had been hard pressed to find amusement in anything; now she found a smile creeping onto her lips. "It must run in the family, then."

He frowned, then seemed to realise he was being teased. "Perhaps it does."

Elizabeth congratulated herself on Darcy's look of surprise the next morning when she stole a moment to announce to him her plan to ride again. He recovered quickly, immediately setting out with her, though she doubted his valet would thank her for taking him to the stable yard without even a change of coat. Still, she was glad of his company; it meant she did not have to pretend to a boldness she did not possess, as she would have to with a stable hand.

He led her around the stable yard again, and Elizabeth counted it as progress that her terror abated enough that she could worry about whether Georgiana would see her foolishness. She was determined to manage three circuits, but by the end of it, her chest was so tight she could not breathe. After she dismounted, she leaned against Pandora's side until her dizziness passed. Darcy said nothing, but she could feel his close gaze on her.

As they walked back to the house, Elizabeth said, "You are very kind to assist me with my riding, but I cannot imagine you are comfortable doing a groom's work."

"My father did it for me when I was first learning to ride. It does not make me uncomfortable. Once I could go beyond the stable yard, my mother gave me lessons."

"Your *mother* taught you to ride?" Elizabeth was startled by this unusual behaviour. Perhaps the Darcy family was not as tradition-bound as she had thought.

"Yes, and Georgiana as well. She was an avid horsewoman. That is why it is so difficult to put restraints on Georgiana's riding; she is riding as our mother did."

"Yet you seem to enjoy riding with her, even when she takes risks."

Darcy paused, dislodging a small rock in the path with his foot and pushing it to the side. "I should not, I know, but sometimes when we are galloping over the grounds, it is as if…"

Elizabeth waited for him to continue, but instead he resumed his normal quick stride. "As if?"

"It is of no importance. You are correct. I ought not encourage her."

Hurt by the dismissal in his voice, Elizabeth said no more. So his civility went no further than the surface. She should not have expected anything else. He had no reason to trust her or to wish to confide in her. At least it *was* civility; that was progress of a sort.

Chapter 9

MRS. REYNOLDS RAN THE household at Pemberley so seamlessly that Elizabeth was rarely called upon for decisions beyond menu selection, so she was surprised when the housekeeper asked to speak to her privately.

"Mrs. Darcy, I have a concern which is beyond my purview. I hope you will not think me interfering."

Elizabeth laid aside her embroidery. "Of course not. Please, continue."

Mrs. Reynolds folded her hands in front of her. "I have a concern for a family here, tenant farmers, not that their farm is producing anything. They appear to be in rather desperate straits. Usually Mr. Dunstan, as steward, would attend to this—he is most dutiful about these matters—but in this particular case, he cannot, as Mr. Tanner refuses any assistance. He does not even allow his wife to speak to her family or friends. From what the children say, there is not enough food, and many of their possessions have been sold to pay for—forgive me, madam—drink. Mrs. Tanner is approaching her confinement and may be ill. No one knows for certain."

"A disturbing situation, indeed. Is there a way I might be of assistance?" Elizabeth felt for the unknown woman at the mercy of a drunken husband and with little recourse. The fingers of her right hand unconsciously sought out her wedding band. A cruel husband could so easily destroy a woman's life and her children's as well. She had been fortunate in that regard, at least so far.

Mrs. Reynolds looked approving. "It strikes me that the husband could not easily refuse to allow the wife of his landlord to visit or to offer aid."

It would be a way to be of use, something she otherwise lacked. The days wore heavily on her since Darcy had stopped spending time with her apart from her morning ride, and Georgiana's company was uncomfortable at best. "I could certainly try. Would it perhaps be better if I called on other families in need as well, so as not to single the Tanners out?"

"An excellent idea, madam. I am certain Mr. Dunstan would have some suggestions."

Over the next hours, Elizabeth found herself being organised by Mrs. Reynolds as efficiently as the rest of the household. She set out in a phaeton accompanied by one of the footmen, baskets of food and other sundries beside her. She was grateful for the footman's company. The task, which had sounded simple enough when first mentioned, began to make her more nervous as she considered the uncertainty of her reception and the necessity of retaining her authority as mistress of Pemberley no matter the circumstances. Perhaps she should have sought Darcy's advice before undertaking the effort.

She chose to visit the tenants with simpler situations first: a new infant, an ill child, a recent death. She had made similar charity visits at Longbourn, though it seemed odd to call upon complete strangers. It helped her regain some of her old assurance. To the Pemberley tenants, her connections did not make her second rate, and they were proud to have Mrs. Darcy call. It had been so long since anyone had been glad to see her, Elizabeth could not help but find some comfort in their pleasure. The newborn babe, bound in coarse swaddling, his baby hair soft against her cheek, did not judge her. The tenants were charmed by her smiles and her easy ways.

Her trepidation increased as they approached the Tanner cottage. Signs of poor maintenance showed even on the outside: ragged thatch, cracks in the timbers, a path growing over with weeds. Only the small vegetable garden appeared cared for. Summoning a mantle of confidence, Elizabeth knocked at the ill-hung door.

It was opened by a girl of perhaps six, clad in a faded and stained dress, with signs of careful mending. Her eyes widened when she saw Elizabeth, and she scampered back inside without a word. A moment later, a woman appeared in the doorway, her hollow cheeks a contrast to the roundness of her body. It was clear she was not far from her confinement. She glanced nervously over Elizabeth's shoulder, as if watching for someone.

Elizabeth introduced herself while the footman carried in a basket of food and sundries. The tenant homes she had seen so far were small but well kept. This one offered little in the way of furniture, and that in poor state.

Two little boys toddled up to her curiously. Elizabeth spoke to them in a friendly tone. "Do you like gingerbread?"

The older of the two, who could not have been above four years of age, glanced uncertainly at his mother. Elizabeth could not help but be disturbed at the degree of anxiety in such a small child.

"When I was your age, I adored it, so I brought some along in case you liked it as well." She produced several pieces and held them out. Each of the boys snatched one, and the older girl crept cautiously closer as Elizabeth offered her one with a smile. The children stuffed the treat into their mouths as if they expected to have it snatched away at any moment.

Elizabeth dusted off her hands. "Well, I can see you do not hate it. Shall I bring more the next time I come?"

"Yes, please," the girl whispered.

Mrs. Tanner expressed hesitant gratitude for the food Elizabeth had brought. "Especially for the children," she said.

"You must eat, too." Elizabeth suspected she might be going hungry in favour of her children. "Is there anything in particular you might find helpful?"

"Thank you kindly, Mrs. Darcy, but we will manage." Her eyes slid away.

Elizabeth remembered Mrs. Reynolds's words about Mr. Tanner selling their possessions for drink. If that were the case, there would be little point in bringing blankets to replace the tattered ones on the bed. Food might be the only assistance she could offer.

Elizabeth wondered whether Darcy would question her tenant visits, but when he said nothing, she followed his lead and did not mention her activities. She developed a routine of visitation every second day, becoming a familiar sight among the small farms of Pemberley. She varied the households she visited but always ended with the Tanners. By the third time she called at the house, the children came running to her for their sweets and no longer seemed so desperate to eat them immediately. Mrs. Tanner rarely said anything beyond thanking Elizabeth for her generosity, but her eyes showed deep gratitude as well as the ever-present fear. Elizabeth understood it better after one occasion when she discovered bruises on Mrs. Tanner's face and arms. It infuriated Elizabeth, but there was nothing to be done for it. She never saw Mr. Tanner; it was as if he did not exist.

Mrs. Reynolds referred to the visits as Mrs. Darcy's charitable activities, but Elizabeth could not think of it as charity. The truth of the matter was that she was happier when visiting the tenants than at any other time. She gave them much needed food and sundries, but they gave her something even more valuable—respect and admiration. As she grew to know the children better, the casual affection they gave her was like water in the desert.

Some of her growing confidence showed to her new family as well. Although she continued to keep her innermost thoughts her own, she made a greater effort to show interest in Georgiana's activities. It became easier with the passage of days and weeks for her to act almost naturally with Mr. Darcy. She became bolder in the stable yard as well, holding her own reins as she made slow circuits on Pandora.

Finally, the day came when she pronounced herself ready to venture beyond the stable yard. Darcy immediately asked for one of his horses to be saddled—not Hurricane, Elizabeth noted, but one she had not seen before, a handsome Arabian, large but placid in appearance.

"Where would you like to go?" Darcy asked.

Elizabeth considered where the ground was most even. "Perhaps around the lake." It was farther than she would rather go this first time, but she hoped Darcy would be pleased by her initiative.

Although they set out at a sedate walk, Elizabeth's hands clutched the reins. From time to time, she glanced at Darcy. He looked perfectly at ease in the saddle, as always, and seemed to spend most of his time watching her rather than the path they were taking. Elizabeth eyed the ground with some anxiety, relaxing only a little when they reached the soft grasses of the bank.

They were near the stone bridge on the far side of the lake when Darcy said, "One of my favourite spots is nearby. If you like, I can show you it, but we would have to leave the horses here."

Elizabeth hesitated, unsure she wished to prolong the ride. But it seemed rude to refuse, so she said she would be happy to see it.

Darcy dismounted with graceful ease and tied his horse's reins to a sapling. He came alongside Pandora just as Elizabeth was contemplating the unpleasant prospect of reaching the ground without the assistance of the mounting block. Without asking her permission, he placed his hands on her waist.

A brief panic overtook her. What if she lost her balance without the stability of the mounting block? She caught at Darcy's shoulders as he lifted her down. It was not until her feet had rested safely on the ground for some moments that she could breathe easily enough to release her grip. Darcy looked down at her with an odd expression, but he let his hands slip off her waist without a word. She could still feel the warmth of his touch.

"Come," he said, "It is this way, through the trees."

She followed him to a grassy bank where the brook tumbled merrily over a series of small cascades before losing itself in the depths of the pond. She had seen the same spot from the other side of the lake countless times, but its charm was not apparent from a distance. She bent down and let the cold water run over her fingers then turned to Darcy with a smile. "It is very soothing," she said. "I wonder where the stream begins."

He pointed to the north. "It has its source in the peaks yonder. The Lambton road follows the valley it has carved over the years."

"Such a small stream to have created such a passage! Your knowledge of the landscape never fails to surprise me."

"It is my home." He seated himself on the grass above her and gestured for her to join him.

She complied, though it made her heart beat faster. It had not escaped her notice that this was the first time since their quarrel they had been alone together in a place where no servants or grooms could be expected to interrupt them. His recent amiability, she knew, must have a goal. The matter of an heir to Pemberley must be in his mind. Certainly he could demand his rights in that regard at any point, but she was beginning to understand that was not in his character. She did not know how it might come about, but she had long since decided when he did approach her, she would greet him with as much civility as she could muster. Still, the uncertainty of it was something she thought of often, and she wondered if he intended to test the waters with her today.

She was taken quite by surprise when he said, "Tell me about your eldest sister."

Elizabeth looked away, remembering the last time Jane's name had arisen between them. She did not want a repeat of their quarrel. "Jane? She is always patient, always kind. She thinks the best of everyone, no matter how telling the evidence against them."

"You are close to her?"

"I was." She remembered her discussion with Jane the night before her wedding. No, since her engagement, she could not claim to be close to Jane.

"But no longer? Why not?"

She hesitated, not wanting to mention his prohibition on writing to her family. Apart from the matter of the Gardiners' visit, he had never said anything further about her correspondence, and she had not wanted to risk asking. "She is in Hertfordshire and I am here. Also, Jane has been unhappy of late and not prone to confidences."

Darcy stood and moved restlessly to the edge of the lake. Picking up a long stick, he swished it through the water. "Why is she unhappy?" His tone was guarded.

"Must we discuss this?" she asked impulsively. "I would rather enjoy the day." Not that she was likely to be at ease with another ride ahead of her.

"Elizabeth, I observed your sister closely on the evening of the ball at Netherfield. Her look and manners were open, cheerful, and engaging, but I perceived no symptoms of peculiar regard for Bingley. She seemed to receive his attentions with pleasure but with no evidence of attachment." He spoke as if his impressions were well-accepted facts.

"There was an attachment. Jane's feelings, though fervent, are little displayed." She tried to speak as calmly as possible, but too many lonely days spent worrying over Jane's unhappiness made it difficult.

He walked up and down the bank in silence then said, "I

must have been in error, then. Your knowledge of your sister is indubitably the superior."

The acknowledgement must have come at some cost to such a proud man, but Elizabeth could not help thinking it was too late to help Jane. She remembered Jane's sadness after Bingley's departure and her own anger. "Jane is not mercenary."

Darcy's lips tightened. "I may have acted in error, but it was done for the best. I did not want Bingley to suffer a marriage where his regard was not returned."

Silence spread like ripples on the lake. Elizabeth averted her eyes, knowing there was nothing she could say in reply. He had not wished that fate on Bingley, and he had taken it on himself instead.

"Perhaps we ought to return now," Darcy said brusquely. He offered Elizabeth his hand to help her to her feet, but there was no warmth in his expression. The curl of his lip suggested he was offering his assistance only because he must and not out of any desire to do so.

Elizabeth followed him back to the horses without a word. They had been doing so well and now this. Surely this could not be the end of their civility! She sought desperately for some response which might alleviate the tension, but watching the set of his shoulders as he strode ahead of her, she decided it would be wiser to say nothing now.

When she reached Pandora's side, she realised that she still lacked the mounting block. She examined the mare's chestnut flanks as if she might find another answer there until she heard Darcy's footsteps behind her.

"I fear I will need your assistance to reach the saddle," she said apologetically.

His only response was to place his hands on her waist and

lift her to the saddle once more. It was fortunate Pandora was so small.

Ignoring her thanks, he mounted his horse and started off down the path. Pandora followed her stable mate's lead, which was fortunate, since Elizabeth felt unequal to putting her lessons in horsemanship to the test. She could find no relief for her sense of loss.

He made no effort to converse as they continued their way back, and Elizabeth was grateful to see the stables coming into view. She did not realise until she dismounted at the block that, in her distress over their discussion, she had not given a second thought to her fear of riding. Excitedly, she turned to Darcy, wanting to share this success with him, but his back was to her. Her courage failed her as she heard him brusquely ask the stable boy to saddle Hurricane.

She could not face him. Instead, she collected Pandora's reins and led her towards the stable. One of the stable hands offered to take her, but Elizabeth shook her head. At Pandora's stall, Elizabeth removed her bridle and found a wizened apple. The horse took the treat from her happily then whickered in her ear.

She saw Hurricane being led past on his way to Darcy. With a shiver of something that might have been pain, Elizabeth buried her face in Pandora's mane, letting the horse's warmth comfort her.

It was nearly suppertime and Elizabeth had yet to see her husband since their ride in the morning. She had watched without success for his return, although she did not know what she would say when she saw him again. She was not yet equal to seeking him out, but when one of the maids came in to offer her refreshment, Elizabeth asked whether Mr. Darcy had arrived back from his ride.

"Madam, begging your pardon, the master's horse came back without him."

"Without him?" cried Elizabeth. "Then where is *he?*"

The maid shrugged helplessly. "That is all I know, please, madam."

Elizabeth frowned. "Would you tell Mrs. Reynolds I would like to speak to her?" The maid curtseyed and left.

Elizabeth's eyes drifted to the window. What could have happened? She had never trusted that stallion. What if Darcy had been thrown and was injured, or worse than injured? She stood and went to the window.

She was still gazing out when Mrs. Reynolds arrived. "You wished to see me, madam?"

"Yes, Mrs. Reynolds. I am told Mr. Darcy's horse returned without him," said Elizabeth, her voice tight. "Do you know anything of this?"

"Only that the horse returned some two hours past, and there is no sign of injury on it."

"*Two hours past!*" Elizabeth cried. "Why was I not informed?"

"We thought it best not to worry you, madam. Mr. Darcy is an excellent horseman, and I do not doubt he dismounted for some reason and the horse ran off."

Elizabeth took a deep breath. "Even the finest of horsemen can take a fall. We must arrange a search for him. He could be injured."

"Mr. Dunstan sent out all the available men as soon as he heard, but it is only a precaution, madam. I am certain myself Mr. Darcy will walk in at any moment demanding his dinner."

Despite the housekeeper's reassuring words, Elizabeth was

certain Mrs. Reynolds was worried as well. She herself knew an anxiety verging on panic.

She had never mentioned to Darcy that the man she saw fall from horseback all those years ago had not survived the incident. She could still remember the whole episode as if it were yesterday—the arc his body made flying through the air, the horrible cracking sound when he struck the ground, and the blood gushing from a wound in his skull then slowing to a standstill a few minutes later as the life left his body. She had been terrified and ran home in a panic. Unable to stop crying, she had been sent to bed where Hill had brought her a posset; Elizabeth had never been able to abide the taste of one since.

What if Darcy were lying out in the hills, bleeding out his last? Wrapping her arms around herself, she began to pace. The mere idea she might never speak to him again, never see his smile or the warmth his eyes sometimes held when he looked at her made her heart pound. The fear was exactly calculated to make her recognise her own wishes.

She did not want to forget the past three months; she wanted to start them over again with the knowledge she now possessed. What might this time have been like had she loved Darcy from the first? If he never returned, she might never even have a chance to tell him. Oh, the opportunities she had wasted!

She crossed to the window again, but the glare of the setting sun made it impossible to see anything on the steep hills surrounding Pemberley.

Chapter 10

IT WAS MORE TO avoid the appearance of impropriety than any desire for food that caused Elizabeth to join Georgiana for supper. It was difficult to make conversation when her thoughts were occupied by Darcy's continued absence.

"Elizabeth, there is no cause for alarm. Fitzwilliam is an excellent horseman and knows what he is about." Georgiana's voice was cool.

Elizabeth pushed her meat around on her plate with her fork. "I hope you are correct. I cannot help but worry."

"Why?"

Somehow she knew the question did not refer to why she felt he was in danger, but rather why it would trouble her if something happened to him. Was this some of the same sort of odd frankness Darcy possessed or Georgiana's own bitterness? She would never have said such a thing were her brother present. Elizabeth took a sip of wine to give herself time to formulate a response. "Appearances are sometimes deceptive, Georgiana. I care about your brother a great deal."

Georgiana's face expressed her scepticism. "If it is any consolation, Fitzwilliam would have made certain you were well provided for."

After hours of worry over Darcy, Elizabeth was roused to an unusual resentment. Without a word, she rang the bell. When one of the maids entered, Elizabeth said, "Would you ask Mr. Dunstan to attend me?"

The maid curtsied and departed. Elizabeth ate a few bites of food she could barely taste until the steward arrived.

Mr. Dunstan was young for his position, only a year or two older than Mr. Darcy, though at the moment his visage was lined with anxiety. "Mrs. Darcy, Miss Darcy. I regret to inform you we have not yet located Mr. Darcy. I have men searching the estate and the roads to Lambton and Matlock."

"Thank you, Mr. Dunstan." Elizabeth, her breath catching in her chest at his words, had almost forgotten why she had asked for him. "Please let me know the moment you hear anything."

"Of course, madam."

Elizabeth glanced at Georgiana. "While you are here, Mr. Dunstan, perhaps you could reassure Miss Darcy on a much more minor matter. She seems concerned that my pin money might be inadequate to my needs, although I have assured her this is not the case."

"By no means, Miss Darcy. Mrs. Darcy's pin money is quite generous, and she spends almost none of it, apart from her charitable work. Even that need not come from her personal funds, and I have often told her, for it is an estate expense. Still, she prefers it this way. You need have no concern."

Georgiana lifted her chin. "Thank you. That will be all."

The door had barely closed behind him when Elizabeth dropped her napkin on the table and pushed her chair back. "I do not care if I am well provided for. I have lived as the daughter of a country gentleman of no particular means, and I would have no difficulty returning to that state. *I* have no need for new pianofortes, expensive gifts, music masters, and paid companions. I will thank you to recall it." Her skirts rustled as she rose, turning her back as she left on Georgiana's frozen countenance.

⁂

The day turned to twilight and twilight to full dark. Elizabeth grew more hopeless as each hour passed, wondering whether she had realised the truth of her feelings for Darcy too late. The house was silent; even the footmen and the cook's boys were out searching by lantern light. There was nothing she could do but fret. Mrs. Reynolds quietly brought a glass of wine and set it beside her, but it remained untouched.

Hearing a noise outside, Elizabeth hurried to see if there was any news. Through the door she heard Darcy's irritable voice. "Leave off. I *will* walk in." Tears of relief sprang to her eyes as she opened the door.

By the light of handheld lanterns, she could make out his familiar figure standing beside a horse she did not recognise and holding its saddle for support while three men stood around him. His coat was torn and muddy.

She hurried down the steps. "Are you hurt?"

"It is nothing." He let go of the horse and one of the men moved closer, as if ready to support him. Darcy turned a glare on him. "I *can* walk."

Elizabeth caught the manservant's eye. "Gentlemen, if you will be so kind as to assist Mr. Darcy to his bedchamber," she said in a firmer voice than she would have thought herself capable of at that moment.

"I need no assistance."

She could see he was barely able to stay upright. It would take a substantial injury to bring him to this state. "Nonetheless, you will accept it, if only to humour me."

Darcy frowned but suffered two of the men to support his arms. They made slow progress, Elizabeth following after with pained concern as she saw how stiffly he held himself. It was a struggle to keep her distance when she wanted nothing more than to throw her arms around him.

It seemed an eon before the little procession, now joined by Mrs. Reynolds, reached Darcy's bedroom. Mrs. Reynolds darted ahead to turn down the bed, then assisted the men as they eased Darcy onto it. He was no longer making even a pretence of independence.

Mrs. Reynolds hovered over him. "Where is your injury, Mr. Darcy?"

He gestured to his left side, wincing as the men tugged off his boots. Ferguson, Darcy's valet, appeared and shooed them aside.

The housekeeper said, "The apothecary has been sent for, sir, but we will need to expose the wound for cleansing."

"Do what you must," Darcy said irritably, "but I need no crowd present."

Mrs. Reynolds, looking disapproving, dismissed the servants, apart from Ferguson. Darcy's eyes turned to Elizabeth. "You should not be here, Elizabeth."

She came forward then and sat on the bed at his right side,

tracing the lines of his countenance with her eyes. "Please do not send me away. I have been so worried." She laid her hand on his and thought her heart might break when he turned his hand over to grasp hers. Perhaps it was not too late. Tears started in her eyes, and their gazes locked, at least until Ferguson began to peel away his riding coat from his injured side. Then Darcy clenched his teeth, looking as if he could barely hold back a cry.

His shirt was stained with blood, both the rich red of fresh blood and a dried brown crust around the edge. A rent in the fabric revealed torn flesh, but how extensive the wound might be Elizabeth could not tell. Darcy's breath hissed through his teeth.

Mrs. Reynolds materialised on the other side of the bed with a glass half filled with amber liquid. "Mr. Darcy, I have laudanum for you."

He grimaced. "I want no laudanum."

"Sir, you will need it for when we clean your wound."

"No. It dulls my mind." Lines of pain etched his face.

Mrs. Reynolds looked at Elizabeth, who held out her hand for the glass. She smoothed a stray lock of hair from his sweat-beaded forehead. "Please, Fitzwilliam. It would ease my mind to know you have less discomfort."

He turned his dark eyes to her, and she squeezed his hand. "Very well," he said grudgingly. Raising his head, he took the glass and drained it. "Vile stuff."

"Thank you," Elizabeth said softly. She wiped the moisture from his brow with her handkerchief.

He closed his eyes, but she could tell by his clenched jaw his pain had not eased.

"Is there anything I can do, anything I can bring you for your comfort?" she asked.

"Talk to me."

"Very well. What shall I talk about?" The only subject on her mind was not one she could raise in front of servants.

"Anything." He winced as he drew in a deep breath.

"I hate your horse."

The shadow of a smile crossed his lips. "Tell me something new."

"That *is* new. I was always frightened of him, but now I hate him as well."

"I am glad to see…" He coughed, half-rising as the movement pained him. "I am glad to see you do not hesitate to speak your mind."

"I do not, and I still hate your horse."

He opened his eyes and looked at her. "I could find another horse, but any horse I choose is likely to be spirited. I prefer them that way."

She surprised herself by lifting his hand and brushing a kiss across his dirt-stained knuckles. "Are there no spirited horses who know when to listen to their riders?"

"No doubt there are." He brought their clasped hands back to his chest. "Are there any further points you wish to argue?" Despite his words, he did not sound troubled.

She could feel his heart beating rapidly underneath her hand. If only the laudanum would take effect, they could discover the extent of his wound. But what if it were something she preferred not to know? What if it was even now too late? She distracted herself by leaning down to kiss his cheek then whispered archly in his ear, "You prefer it when I argue with you."

"My secret is discovered." His speech was beginning to slur.

Elizabeth heard the snipping sound of scissors cutting cloth.

Mrs. Reynolds exposed the wound and began to apply wet poultices to it. Darcy tensed at each touch, attempting to watch the proceedings.

"May I assist?" Elizabeth asked.

Mrs. Reynolds shook her head without looking up. "Distraction will help more than anything else."

Elizabeth moved closer to Darcy and clasped his hand in both her own. "Where were you when this happened?"

"Near Curbar Edge." He winced.

She put her hand to his face. "Fitzwilliam, look at me. Try to remain still."

"I am…" his breath caught, "…at your command."

"How did you injure yourself?" The metallic odour of blood permeated the air.

"Too close an acquaintance with one of the boulders you so admire. Hurricane took a sudden dislike to a wildcat."

"A wildcat?" She had not realised such animals lived in the hills of Derbyshire.

"Yes. It inspected me afterwards but decided I was not sufficiently appetising to be worth its trouble. But it was enough to convince me to begin walking back."

His mind was evidently beginning to wander. Elizabeth glanced down and gasped. The wound encompassed most of his side, fragments of torn muscle showed through, and crusted blood was everywhere.

Mrs. Reynolds said, "It is not too deep from what I can see. I suspect he has lost a great deal of blood, but I do not believe the wound itself is grave. If it does not fester, it should heal well."

Elizabeth let out a sobbing breath of relief. Darcy did not

stir, his even breathing indicating he was asleep. Now she no longer fought to hold back tears, despite the presence of Mrs. Reynolds and Ferguson. She could not bear to look at the ragged wound.

A knock sounded at the door. Ferguson answered it, then turned to Elizabeth. "Miss Darcy, madam."

Elizabeth dashed the tears from her eyes then took herself into the hallway where Georgiana stood. Darcy would not want his sister to see his injury.

Georgiana looked pale in the dim light. "What has happened? Mr. Dunstan says he is injured."

"A flesh wound only, but he is weak from loss of blood. He is asleep now, thanks to laudanum. He will no doubt be happy to see you when he awakens."

"Will he…" The girl swallowed hard.

"There appears to be no immediate danger. I will send you word if there is any change."

"Thank you." Georgiana clenched her hands at her sides as Elizabeth reached for the door handle. "Elizabeth?"

"Yes?"

"I apologise for what I said earlier. There is much I do not know."

Elizabeth could see her tension and wished she knew better how to support her in this crisis. In this, Georgiana was as alone as she was. Elizabeth touched the girl's arm lightly. "It is forgotten. I hope we will understand one another better in future."

Elizabeth did not stir from her husband's room that night. At first she simply watched him sleep, comforting herself with the sight of his features by the dim light of a lamp turned low. How could she not have realised what he had come to mean to her? In hindsight, it seemed perfectly incomprehensible, yet in truth, it had begun so gradually that she was in the middle before she knew it had begun.

Mrs. Reynolds had offered to have a servant stay with him through the night, but Elizabeth had refused, unable to bear being parted from him. She could not explain it, but somehow it felt as if his recovery depended on her presence, as if her previous failures as a wife demanded she make every effort now. When her eyelids began to droop, she removed her slippers and lay down on the bed beside him.

It was still dark when she awoke from a restless slumber to find Darcy muttering and pulling at his bandages. Clearly, he was still in pain and somewhat confused, so she prepared another dose of laudanum for him from the bottle Mrs. Reynolds had left for that purpose. Eventually, it allowed him to sleep again, but this time he held onto her, his good arm curved around her, his fingers tangled in her hair. She wished she could press her body against his to reassure herself of the reality of his survival, but she was afraid of causing him further pain.

<hr />

Elizabeth awoke when the first streaks of light began to brighten the sky. Careful not to disturb her husband, she slipped out of his bed and resumed her earlier position in the chair. Even in sleep, she could see the lines of pain in Darcy's face.

She left his room only for her toilette, instructing Ferguson to call her immediately should Darcy wake up and urging Lucy to hurry with a clean dress. Being away from his bedside made her profoundly nervous, and she was relieved to find him still sleeping when she returned.

His eyes did not open until Mrs. Reynolds attempted to change his blood-soaked bandages. He winced in pain, but no sound escaped him.

Elizabeth took his hand in hers. "I would say good morning, but I fear you would rather be asleep again."

"It is not so bad as that." His words were belied by the painfully tight grip he had on her hand.

On the other side of the bed, Mrs. Reynolds measured out another dose of laudanum.

"We have sent to Matlock for the doctor. We trust he will be here today."

"I do not need a doctor. A little rest is all I require." He made a face at the bitter taste of the drug. "Have you been here all night?"

The lock of hair had fallen onto his forehead again, and she gently touched it. "Yes, I have been keeping you company."

He glanced at Mrs. Reynolds, then motioned to Elizabeth to come closer. She leaned down to hear his whisper.

"Elizabeth, you need not be here... for this."

She stroked his hand, still entwined with her own. "I want to be with you."

His mouth twisted in a wry line. "There is a first time for everything."

Hot tears pricked at the corners of her eyes. "Please, Fitzwilliam. Until you disappeared, I did not realise how dear to me you have become."

His eyes widened. "Is that the truth or an attempt to please me?"

"The truth. I cannot believe how foolish I have been," she murmured in his ear. She wished they were alone so she could tell him much more.

He turned his face towards hers. "It is I who have been foolish. Had I but known…"

She could hear the agitation in his voice. "Sh, my love. That is all past, and you must concentrate your strength on recovering from your injury."

The corners of his lips turned up. "Yes, indeed I must, though, it is worth the injury to have a welcome such as this."

"Do not say such things. I only want you well again."

His eyelids drifted downwards. "And to think laudanum usually gives me nightmares, not sweet dreams."

He faded in and out of sleep as the day went on. Elizabeth kept her hand clasped in his, even when she read to him and had to balance the open book on her lap to turn the pages. He did not seem to object, and for her part, she could not be close enough to him.

She stayed with him through the night again. This time her fatigue made her sleep more soundly, but she still woke every time Darcy stirred, and she continued her vigil in the morning.

Towards afternoon, she looked up from her book to see his dark eyes watching her.

"Elizabeth." His voice sounded rough as if with disuse.

She shifted to sit on the bed beside him. "Yes? Can I bring you anything?"

"Just yourself."

Elizabeth smiled. "I am here, my love."

He reached out his good arm. "Come lie beside me."

It was broad daylight, but they were alone. It would not hurt to do as he asked, and it would comfort her as well. "As you wish."

He put his arm around her, seemingly content with her presence. Elizabeth wished she dared to hold him, but she was afraid of hurting him. But when he turned his head sideways on the pillow, his eyes clouded with the drug, she leaned towards him to meet his lips with her own. It was a gentle kiss, but his lips were hot against hers. Elizabeth almost shook with the emotion of it. Finally, they were where they ought to have been all along.

But gradually, it impinged on her consciousness that his mouth was warmer than desire could account for. She put her hand to his forehead. Burning hot.

Panic gripped her throat. She knew full well the danger of a fever in such a situation. His wound must be festering. "You have a fever. I must call for Mrs. Reynolds."

"No, stay with me."

She could see he did not comprehend the gravity of the situation. The pupils of his eyes were shrunk almost to nothing. "I will return immediately, as soon as I send word."

"You will not leave me when the servants come?" She could hear the anxiety in his voice, echoing her own deeper fear.

She kissed his forehead. "I will not leave you, I promise."

Chapter 11

IT BECAME A NIGHTMARE of blurred days and nights. The doctor called each day and said the same thing, that Mr. Darcy was young and healthy, and the fever might run its course. On the third day of his fever, Elizabeth penned brief letters to his uncle and to Colonel Fitzwilliam informing them of his condition. Her chest ached as she wrote.

Mrs. Reynolds continued to give Darcy laudanum to prevent him from reopening the wound as he thrashed in pain. Elizabeth did not leave his bedside, catching little bits of sleep either in the chair or near him on the bed; but she was never asleep long before she awakened with the taste of fear in her mouth. She could not lose him now.

Darcy would wake from time to time. Sometimes he knew her and sometimes he did not, but she always told him she loved him. There might not be another chance. One time, he took Mrs. Reynolds for his mother, bringing tears to the housekeeper's eyes.

Another time he looked at her with furrowed brows. "You ought not be here, Miss Bennet. Where is my aunt?" His speech was slurred.

"Your aunt?"

"Lady Catherine," he said irritably.

She touched his forehead. Still hot. "We are at Pemberley, not Rosings, and we are married, my love."

"Oh." He turned his head from side to side, as if to clear it. "Married? Are you certain?"

"Quite certain. Look, here is Ferguson, and he will tell you so."

"Indeed, Mr. Darcy. Mrs. Darcy is quite correct. You are injured and have a fever."

"And we are married?" He seemed to find this quite astonishing.

Elizabeth held out her hand so her wedding band was visible. "Quite indelibly, sir." She would not say *Till death us do part*.

"Oh. That is well, then." His face seemed to relax, and his eyes drifted shut again.

There were more hours of placing cool cloths on his forehead, of checking the swollen red flesh around his wound, of trying to convince him to take sips of broth and the remedies the apothecary had provided. Georgiana came in each morning and evening and sat with him briefly, unable to stay long without sobbing uncontrollably. Elizabeth offered her what consolation she could; Georgiana's attitude towards her had changed considerably since the day of Darcy's accident.

Colonel Fitzwilliam arrived at Pemberley three days after she sent her letters. He had ridden posthaste from London and came directly to Darcy's sickbed before he had even changed out of his dusty riding coat. As usual, Darcy was in a restless sleep.

The colonel did not mince words. "Has he shown any improvement?"

Elizabeth was too tired to stand when he entered and too worried to care about this breach of etiquette. "Very little, I fear.

His fever continues, and he is growing weaker with time. He is often confused and has no interest in food or drink."

"What does the doctor say?"

Elizabeth closed her eyes for a moment before she answered. "He says Mr. Darcy's youth and healthy constitution are our best hopes."

Colonel Fitzwilliam snorted. "Doctors."

Darcy's eyes fluttered open. "Richard?" His voice was little more than a whisper.

"At your service." Colonel Fitzwilliam placed his arm under Darcy's shoulders, lifting him partway from the bed. "Darcy, you must drink." He motioned to Elizabeth for a cup.

Darcy shook his head weakly. "Not thirsty."

The colonel's voice hardened. "Drink this, or I will drag you out to the old stable and thrash you soundly."

Elizabeth stared at him in shock, but her husband obediently sipped the broth. His cousin held the cup for him patiently then wiped the corner of his mouth when he was done. Darcy's eyes drifted closed, and the colonel eased him down on his pillow. "You may rest a moment but then you must sit up."

"But he cannot sit," Elizabeth objected.

"He will sit, and later we will get him to his feet. I have seen my share of festering wounds, and the ones who lie abed do not recover. He must use his body, no matter how weak it may be."

Elizabeth nodded. She had no idea if it was true, but she would take any hope. "Tell me what I should do."

"No, thank you. I will have a tray here, I think." Elizabeth, in her accustomed seat at Darcy's bedside, did not pause in her embroidery.

Colonel Fitzwilliam frowned. "Elizabeth, go down to dinner. I will stay with him."

"Thank you, but I prefer to stay here."

"You will not help him by making yourself ill. Georgiana, tell her."

Georgiana stepped forward. "He is right, Elizabeth. Please, come away for at least a few minutes."

Elizabeth looked up in surprise at the genuine concern in the girl's voice. "I appreciate the sentiment, but truly, I am perfectly well here."

The colonel crossed his arms. "Elizabeth, either you go down to dinner with Georgiana of your own accord, or I will wake your husband and have *him* tell you to do it."

"You would not! He needs his rest." Elizabeth recognised his implacable look, the same one he used so effectively on Darcy. It was definitely a new side of the gentleman she knew. "Very well, since you insist. But I will return after dinner."

"The change will do you good," Georgiana said earnestly.

Elizabeth laid aside the embroidery. She did not want to add to Georgiana's worries. She forced a smile to her face. "You are right. I should take more care."

⁂

"Up you go," Colonel Fitzwilliam urged, with a hand on Darcy's shoulder.

Darcy opened his eyes. "Not you again, Richard."

"You were about to sit up, Darcy. Now," he said sharply. With Ferguson's help, he assisted Darcy to a sitting position.

Darcy's face was tight with pain. "Good." Supporting his cousin's back, Colonel Fitzwilliam looked at Elizabeth with a hint of a smile. "There is something to be said for being three years his elder."

Elizabeth could picture the two men as squabbling boys. "And did you indeed take him out to the old stable and thrash him?"

"Not *often*, and he soon learned to thrash me back." For a moment, he looked like his old amiable self, telling an amusing story.

Darcy began to cough deep, hacking coughs that made him clutch at his side. Colonel Fitzwilliam held his shoulders. "That's right. Cough it up. Get it out of you."

Elizabeth hated seeing him in such discomfort. "Are you sure this is helping him?"

Colonel Fitzwilliam looked across Darcy to her, his countenance more serious than usual. "It is the best I have to offer."

She noticed he had not answered her question.

"Mr. Dunstan, what can I do for you?" Elizabeth was puzzled by the steward's request to speak to her, but Colonel Fitzwilliam had urged her to meet him, no doubt to get her out of the sickroom for a few minutes.

He cleared his throat. "I have a question regarding the estate which requires a timely response."

"I will be happy to help if I can, though I know little of estate management."

"Thank you, madam." He clasped his hands. "It is a matter of poaching. Jack Bridges, who is the youngest son of one of our tenants, was caught taking a rabbit on Pemberley grounds. He could be sent to the magistrate, but this is his first offence, and

Mr. Darcy's custom in such cases has been to suggest some form of restitution instead."

"Is there some reason it would not be suitable in this case?"

"No, madam; it is simply that Mr. Darcy feels such decisions should come from him, not from me. In his illness, I thought it best to bring the matter to you."

Elizabeth could see why it could cause difficulties if the steward were to administer justice on his own. "What would he usually suggest as restitution?"

"For poaching? Most often six months' labour on the estate."

"Six months for a rabbit?"

"Madam, it needs to be a serious enough punishment to deter others, or we would have an epidemic of poaching. It is preferable to expulsion."

"Is the estate in need of labour?"

"Not at the moment, madam, but something can always be found."

Perhaps she should ask Richard to make the decision. If Darcy did not recover, the colonel would be running Pemberley as Georgiana's guardian. She swallowed the lump in her throat. No, she would not allow for that possibility. She would choose for herself.

The safest option would be to do as her husband had done in the past, but she knew the Bridges family from her tenant visits, and they could ill spare the labour on their own farm. Yet there must be some consequence. If she acted as judge, would it affect her position with the tenants? She preferred to be the one who brought them relief rather than punishment.

"Mr. Dunstan, what would you say to this? He must chop firewood for the widow Gibbs for a year and make the needed repairs to her cottage as well as work two days a week at the

Hammond farm until Mr. Hammond's leg is sufficiently healed for him to return to his fields."

The steward's eyebrows shot up, but he quickly resumed his normal expression. "That would no doubt be well received, madam."

"Would you consider that an adequate deterrent? I fear old Mr. Bridges cannot work his land by himself."

"A valid point, madam. I think it would do very well indeed."

"If you would be so kind, I would like to be kept abreast of the developments in this case."

Mr. Dunstan nodded. "If you have time tomorrow, I will let you know the outcome."

"Thank you." She would certainly have time tomorrow; time was all she had. Any distraction would be welcome.

That night, as exhaustion overtook her, she lay down beside Darcy and fell into a sleep of disturbing dreams. In one dream, she was adrift in a small boat with a leak in the bottom. She could do nothing but watch the water creep in, becoming deeper and deeper, until she was soaked to the skin. She awoke to find the sensation was true; there was a salty wetness on her face, and her nightdress, damp where her body touched her husband's, clung to her. She thought at first she must have been crying in her sleep, but then she realised the moisture had a different source. Darcy's body was beaded with perspiration, the sheets around him soaked. Torn between desperate hope and fear, Elizabeth laid her hand against his forehead. His fever had broken.

She returned to her own bed for the first time since his accident, and Ferguson stayed with Darcy. Her first thought when she awoke, refreshed by uninterrupted sleep, was for her husband. She immediately rang for Lucy, who brought the welcome news that his fever had not returned and he had taken a little broth earlier. Eager to see him, she hurried through her toilette, making Lucy laugh at her impatience.

When she arrived at his room, he was asleep again. Taking her accustomed seat beside his bed, she noticed his cheeks no longer had the heightened colour of the previous days and his breathing was easier. She smiled, thinking of the future they would share together.

One time when she glanced up from her embroidery, she found him looking at her, his eyes clear once again. She reached out to take his hand, but he did not respond to her gentle pressure.

"Elizabeth." His voice was gravelly.

"It is good to see you looking better, Fitzwilliam."

"Why are you here?"

Her smile slipped. "To be with you, of course."

He turned his head away, staring up at the canopy. "I want nothing of you."

A chill ran through her. Surely he could not mean it, not after all the hand-holding and whispered intimacies of the last few days? She had been so certain he felt as she did, that all their troubles were in the past. Had it just been his fever and the laudanum speaking? Her skin burnt at the thought of it.

She swallowed hard. "You wish me to leave?"

"Yes. Be gone. And trouble me no more." There was a cold implacability in his expression she remembered from the days after their quarrel, one she had hoped never to see again.

She had forgotten that his ill-fated ride had begun after another disagreement with her, this time over Jane. Apparently, he had not. Stricken, she stood, straightening her skirt before picking up her embroidery. "Should you wish to see me, you need only send word, and I will be happy to attend you."

He said nothing, and she turned to go, but not before noticing Ferguson's sympathetic look. No doubt he was sorry for her, but not so sorry that everyone in the household would not be aware within hours that her husband had dismissed her. She gathered what remained of her dignity and made her way to the adjoining door. She glanced back once at Darcy, the twisted expression on his face only accentuating his pallor. "My best wishes for your recovery, sir."

She closed the door blindly behind her and stumbled across the sitting room to the safety of her own bedroom, where she could give way to the luxury of tears.

Chapter 12

ELIZABETH WENT DOWN TO dinner with high colour in her cheeks, wondering how many of the servants knew she had been banned from her husband's bedside. She would have to accustom herself to the humiliation of it; anyone who was not aware of it already would discover it soon enough. Georgiana and Colonel Fitzwilliam gave no sign of any change in her situation, but perhaps they were just being kind. She managed to choke down only a few bites during a meal which seemed to last for hours, and fortunately, no one showed surprise when she excused herself as soon as it was over.

Her mortification could not still her concern for her husband's health. If only her disgrace had the power to stop her from caring for him! But it was not to be. It was understandable enough that he would reject her overtures now; she had rejected his in the past. Finally, exhausted with the struggle of not knowing, she asked Lucy to have Ferguson wait upon her. She could ask him about Darcy's well-being; he could have no doubts as to why she could not find out for herself.

She had never known one could feel pain through every inch of one's being, but now it became her familiar companion. Was this how Darcy had felt after their argument? If so, it was no surprise he wanted nothing to do with her any longer.

She resumed her tenant visits, giving purpose to her days which otherwise would be full of useless self-reproach. With Mr. Dunstan's advice, she expanded the circle of families she visited and became a familiar figure among the cottages as she brought food to the ailing and the invalids. She was received by them with gratitude. The word of her judgement regarding Jack Bridges had spread, and with it the esteem in which they held her. When she spoke with the people of Pemberley, especially the children, sometimes she could forget her grief for a few minutes, but never for long.

Back at Pemberley House, she threw herself into the task of becoming the best possible mistress of Pemberley. If she could not have Darcy's love, she would do her best to satisfy him in that regard. She learned the names and habits of the plants in the hothouses and took over arranging flowers throughout the house, planned meals in conjunction with the cook, and spent hours practicing on the pianoforte as she had heard Georgiana do. She played in the evenings for Colonel Fitzwilliam and Georgiana; it was easier than conversing with them. She grimly rode Pandora each day accompanied by a stable hand, finding her earlier panic in riding now returning with Darcy's absence. But he had wanted her to learn to ride, and ride she would. If she enjoyed none of it, there was nothing to be done for it. She found no pleasure in anything.

Her only ray of hope was that less than a fortnight remained until the Gardiners were due to arrive. Although her first thought was to disguise any troubles from them, on reflection, she decided she would tell her aunt everything, in the hope that she might have some wisdom to impart. She had nothing left to lose.

From Ferguson's reports she knew that Darcy continued his slow recovery. He relapsed into a fever that lasted several days, and Elizabeth found herself once again unable to sleep at night for worry, even though he was no longer hers to lose.

Elizabeth was practicing her music when Colonel Fitzwilliam strode into the room. She had successfully avoided being alone with him until now, given how Darcy had responded to her behaviour in his presence at his last visit. A cosy tête-à-tête while she played was not in her plans, so she closed the pianoforte and asked him the question most on her mind. "How does my husband?"

"He continues to improve slowly."

"I am glad to hear it."

He lowered himself into a chair and put his legs out in front of him. "I have spent a great deal of time at my cousin's bedside with little to do apart from reflect. I have been wondering why a woman who never left her husband's side during his illness would suddenly absent herself when he started to recover. I confess I am exceedingly puzzled."

Of course her behaviour must look odd if he had not heard the household gossip. She chose her words with care; she did not want him to think too ill of her. "I promised to love, honour, and obey my husband. I believe this would fall under 'obey.'"

"Do you mean to suggest he told you to stay away? I do not believe it."

"I have said all I am prepared to say on this subject." She made a show of choosing a new sheet of music.

"Then I shall ask my cousin himself. Good day, madam."

"No!" She rose to her feet and took a step towards him. "*Please* do not tell him you spoke to me."

Her panic must have communicated itself to him, for he stopped, regarding her with bewilderment. "My dear Elizabeth, there is no cause for alarm. You have said nothing he could object to, and he is a fair man."

She could not tell him of Darcy's suspicions about them. She searched frantically for an explanation which would not discredit her completely. But there was no point. It could not make matters any worse if the colonel disapproved of her. "My husband suspects me of preferring the attention of other men. If he knew we had spoken alone, he would be angry with me."

There was a long, humiliating silence, and finally she looked away. His voice, when it finally came, was carefully neutral. "Is there any truth to his suspicions?"

She rounded on him. "No, of course not!" Her anger leached away as quickly as it had come. Defeated, she said, "As I was unable to convince my husband of it, I doubt I can convince you. But now you are answered; please do not question me further."

"This makes no sense."

"If you will excuse me, Colonel." She slipped out of the room before he could say anything further.

The next day brought a letter from Jane. Elizabeth's eyes misted at her sister's familiar handwriting, although the direction was written ill. She held the letter in her hands as if it somehow contained an essence of Jane. Somewhere there were people who still loved her. Soon, too, she would see the Gardiners.

Finally she opened it, determined to read it slowly and savour every word.

Dearest Lizzy,

Something has occurred of a most unexpected and serious nature; but I am afraid of alarming you—be assured that we are all well. What I have to say relates to poor Lydia. I do not know if you were aware she was spending the summer with her friend Mrs. Forster in Brighton, so she could continue to enjoy the company of the officers in the regiment who had gone thither from Meryton. An express came at twelve last night, just as we were all gone to bed, from Colonel Forster, to inform us that she was gone off to Scotland with one of his officers. Imagine our surprise! To Kitty, however, it does not seem so wholly unexpected. I am very, very sorry. But I am willing to hope for the best. Our poor mother is sadly grieved. My father bears it better. They were off on Saturday night about twelve, as is conjectured, but were not missed till yesterday morning at eight. The express was sent off directly. My dear Lizzy, they must have passed within ten miles of us. Colonel Forster gives us reason to expect him here soon. Lydia left a few lines for his wife, informing her of their intention. I must conclude, for I cannot be long from my poor mother. I am afraid you will not be able to make it out, but I hardly know what I have written.

Elizabeth hardly knew what to think. Lydia had eloped? Surely she could not be so foolish, so careless with the reputation of her family. It would hurt all her sisters' chance of marriage, undoing all the good her own marriage had done to the Bennet family name. Foolish, foolish girl!

Darcy would be furious at this scandal touching him. It would confirm his every prejudice against her family. The heat of shame rushed through her. How could she ever tell him?

She was still debating the question the following day when an express arrived for her. She snatched at the letter on the silver tray, expecting it to be further news from Longbourn. But the writing was not Jane's neat script but a hurried, uneven hand.

Dear Lizzy,

Is this not a marvellous joke? I cannot help laughing myself at your surprise. I venture you did not think when you left Longbourn that I should be the first of your sisters to marry! Just think—I will now go before Jane!

Elizabeth shut her eyes. Lydia had always been heedless, but she would never have thought her sister would sink so low. What had her father been thinking, to allow Lydia to go to Brighton?

But I must stop now, for my dearest Wickham has a question he must ask you.

Lydia

Wickham? Surely he could not have been the one to elope with Lydia. Poor Lydia—bound for life to a man who could not be trusted, whose lies had cost Elizabeth so dearly, the man her husband so detested. It could not be worse; Darcy would never let her see her family again.

The letter continued in a man's clear handwriting.

My dear Elizabeth,

I hope I may take the liberty to address you so informally, now that we are to be sister and brother. I am sure you have already heard the tale of our elopement. Sadly, your dear sister and I are not yet in Scotland, but still in London, held back by an unfortunate shortage of funds. There are many demands in the life of an officer. I cannot in good conscience proceed to wed while outstanding debts of honour await me and without proper means to support a wife. So, dear Elizabeth, I appeal to your generous nature. I believe twelve thousand pounds would be sufficient to settle my debts and to purchase a position in keeping with my married state. I hope you will communicate with me at the direction below so we may resolve this obstacle between ourselves with expediency.

With all best wishes,
G. Wickham

No. He could not possibly have meant it in such a way. That he had lied to her she had accepted, but that he would risk ruining a young girl and suggest such blackmail! It was beyond belief. She scanned the letter again, hoping against hope to discover a different meaning in it. But it was clear enough;

he would only marry Lydia if Elizabeth somehow produced the required sum. Twelve thousand! Did he think Darcy so besotted with her that he would part with so much money? Wickham was due for an unpleasant surprise in that case.

So Lydia would be ruined, and the Bennet family along with her. Tears came to Elizabeth's eyes for her poor, foolish sister and the price Lydia would pay for the rest of her life. It would cost Elizabeth as well. Now there was no hope Darcy would accept her family. The scandal it would bring to the Darcy name would make it impossible. They would have to break all ties to her family. Even then, Darcy would never forgive her this.

There was no hiding from it either. Elizabeth would have to tell him and see the disgust in his eyes. But first, she would take action herself. In that way, at least, she might redeem herself slightly in her husband's eyes.

She crossed to the inlaid writing desk and took out a sheet of paper.

Elizabeth paused outside the door to Darcy's bedroom. Her trepidation of the outcome was so great that it could make no difference what happened; it could be no worse than she imagined—more humiliation and a death knell to any hopes she harboured that Darcy might one day care for her again.

Ferguson opened the door to her knock. She glanced over his shoulder; Darcy was awake, so she had no excuse for delay there.

"Mrs. Darcy," the valet said, holding the door open for her.

"Thank you, Ferguson. I would like to speak to my husband alone."

He bowed. "Of course, madam." He closed the door behind him.

The distance between the doorway and the bed seemed to have lengthened since the last time Elizabeth had walked it. Her husband was half-sitting, propped up with pillows. A lock of dark hair fell over his forehead, and she fought the urge to straighten it. He would not appreciate the gesture.

She sat beside the bed. "You look well today, sir." In truth, his face was even thinner, and it pained her to see it.

"My health continues to improve, I thank you." Darcy's countenance was serious. "I hope you are well."

"I am, but I have news of a most unfortunate nature to discuss with you."

He stiffened slightly, his expression becoming more guarded. "Yes, madam?"

Elizabeth wanted to look away, but she would not be so cowardly. "Yesterday, I received a letter from my sister Jane informing me that my youngest sister had eloped with an officer. It contained no details except that attempts to find her had proved unsuccessful." She handed him the letter, but he did not open it. She took a deep breath. "Today, a letter from Lydia came by express. At least, it purported to be from Lydia; in fact, most of it is written by Mr. Wickham, who makes an offer of an offensive nature." This time he perused the letter immediately, frowning as he did so.

She did not wait for his response. "I have already sent my reply. I told Lydia that under no circumstances would I agree to Mr. Wickham's request; but as I found I could not leave her to live on the streets, I would arrange for a small allowance to be paid to my uncle Gardiner to cover the cost of an anonymous retreat for her. Lastly, I wrote to my sister Jane and asked her to explain to my parents why they would not hear from me again." She was proud of herself; her voice had remained calm even though the pain in her chest was fierce.

"You have heard nothing further?"

"Nothing, sir."

He looked at the letter once more. "Would you be so kind as to inform Colonel Fitzwilliam I wish to speak with him immediately?" His tone was more absent than anything else.

"Of course." All that was left for her was to retire with dignity.

Chapter 13

ELIZABETH FELT TOO LISTLESS to stir from her room at dinnertime. Lucy brought her up a tray of food, though she had not asked for it, along with the news that Colonel Fitzwilliam would be departing at first light. She also brought a letter from Mrs. Gardiner, with the expected news that their Northern tour was indefinitely postponed. The need to remain in London and to search for Lydia took precedence. It did not make her cry; she felt too numb for that. She asked Ferguson to relay the news to Darcy. She did not wish to observe his reaction to the knowledge that he was free of the obligation of the visit.

She penned a quick response, including the direction Wickham had given as a possibility for their search but without a word as to how she came into possession of it. In closing, she sent all her best love and respect, with special messages for each of the children. She sealed it and gave it to Lucy to send before she lost her courage. There was no doubt in her mind that it would be the last communication she would have with them. After this disgrace, even she could see the danger to the

Darcy family name. Her duty was clear, no matter how it tore at her heart.

Now she was truly alone. She had depended so much upon the idea of the Gardiners' visit, not only for the connection to people she cared about, but also for the opportunity to seek her aunt's wisdom about her confusing relationship with Darcy. Well, it was confusing no longer; she knew precisely what he felt.

There was nothing to be done for it. She had lost everything of value to her: her husband's love, her family, her home, and her faith in her own judgement and good sense. The brief taste of happiness she had experienced when she thought Darcy's affection for her was undiminished only made her present state the more bitter.

It was hardest to live with the knowledge of how much she must have hurt him. He had loved her ardently, of that she had no doubt, and now she understood the bitter pain of rejection. How much the worse it must have been for him to have thought he had her affection for those months only to learn the truth! How could she have been so cruel? Her present sufferings were well deserved.

Elizabeth managed a small semblance of a smile for Georgiana when the girl came to see her in her room.

Georgiana's hands were clasped tightly in front of her. "Are you angry with me, Elizabeth?"

"No, of course not." Elizabeth gestured to an empty chair.

The girl shifted uncomfortably. "You have not been down for a meal in two days, so I thought perhaps I had done something to offend you."

"No, indeed." Elizabeth searched for words. "I have been fit company for no one but myself. I beg your pardon for worrying you."

"Is there anything I can do to help?"

Elizabeth looked out the window to avoid Georgiana's eyes. "I suppose there is no point in secrecy, since you will discover it eventually in any case. My youngest sister is lost to us, my family is in disgrace, and I with them."

"Lost to you?" Georgiana exclaimed. "What has happened?"

"An officer convinced her to elope with him. She is young and foolish, but that is no excuse. Her thoughtlessness has ruined my family. It is not the sort of thing that would happen in a family like yours, except that your brother made the unfortunate mistake of marrying me." She did not feel ready to tell Georgiana that this was much worse than a mere elopement.

Georgiana looked down and smoothed her skirts. "Anyone can be young and foolish, no matter how fine their family."

Elizabeth supposed the girl meant it as comfort. "That is kind of you to say, but I cannot believe you would ever find yourself in such a situation."

"You would suppose wrongly, then." Georgiana's voice could scarcely be heard. "Please do not be too vexed with your sister. In all likelihood, she meant no ill."

The very quietness of her voice pulled Elizabeth from her own hopeless misery. Poor Georgiana was clearly troubled. Perhaps she was afraid of what this would do to her own chances or still worried Elizabeth was angry with her. "You are very generous, more so than she deserves."

Georgiana's hands clutched at her skirt, then she stood. "Please excuse me. I must go."

Elizabeth laid her hand on Georgiana's arm. "Is something troubling you?" She might not understand Georgiana, but she could not ignore her distress.

"You would despise me, too, if you knew." Georgiana averted her face but did not try to move away.

"If I knew what?"

"Last year, when I was still young enough to believe in love, there was a man. He was an old family friend, or at least I thought he was. I did not know he and Fitzwilliam had fallen out. He told me he loved me and convinced me to go to Scotland with him. I knew I ought not, that it was wrong, but people make fools of themselves for love. I would have gone had not Fitzwilliam discovered it and stopped me. I cannot bear to think what I almost put him through."

Elizabeth's heart went out to her. "Please, sit down. You must not blame yourself for trusting a man who loved you."

"He did not love me. He only wanted my fortune. He admitted as much in the end." She spoke bitterly but resumed her seat.

"Oh, my dear. I am so sorry."

"It taught me a valuable lesson. Love causes nothing but pain. The next time, I will know what a man who says he loves me truly wants. How could I be fool enough to believe anything else of George Wickham? He had nothing, no money, the lowest of connections."

The name stopped Elizabeth short. "George Wickham? He was the man who did this?"

Georgiana paled. "You know of him?"

"I have met him. He is the officer with whom my sister has eloped." Their eyes met in shared horror.

So tricking young girls into believing they loved him was not something new for Wickham, nor was trying to manoeuvre his way into obtaining Darcy's money. Had he targeted Lydia because of Elizabeth's marriage to Darcy? Was this, too, her fault?

"I am very sorry. I hope it works out for the best for your sister."

"Thank you, though I doubt the outcome can be good. Still, I hope you do not let one selfish man keep you from believing in love."

Georgiana's mouth twisted. "I believe it exists, though rarely. What I doubt is my ability to recognise it, when the majority of gentlemen who express interest in me only care about my fortune."

No wonder Georgiana had been so ready to believe her a fortune hunter. Elizabeth wondered if her husband had been as cynical about love before meeting her. And she had taken his precious gift and trampled it in the mud.

⚜

Elizabeth made a rare outing into the park, seeking to walk off her restlessness. She was returning to the house when she saw the carriage drawn up in front of the house. Darcy stood beside it, his normally excellently fitting coat now hanging on his thinner form. Despite everything, she was glad to see him. She had not realised he had recovered enough to leave his rooms.

Two servants carried a trunk to the carriage and loaded it on the back. Darcy reached for the carriage door and a footman supported his arm.

Elizabeth picked up her skirt and ran to the carriage. "You are not leaving?"

Darcy stepped up into the carriage. He leaned back against the cushion, looking tired, before responding. "Yes, I am. You need not worry."

"But you are not well enough to travel!"

"I am beyond any danger." Darcy's eyes flickered over her shoulder, drawing her attention to the servants behind her. Elizabeth drew in a half-sobbing breath. He was leaving, and she did not know where he was going or why.

Elizabeth's concern overrode her caution. "Please, if you must travel, can you not wait to regain your strength?"

"Elizabeth." He looked at her significantly. "You know why I must go."

Suddenly, the realisation came to her. He was leaving because of her, so he need not be reminded continually of the error he had made in marrying her. Her chest grew so tight she could barely breathe. She took a step backwards and looked down at the ground, unable to meet his eyes. "Of course," she said dully. "Forgive me for troubling you." She wanted to tell him not to take any risks with his health, but he would not wish to hear it. "I hope your journey is safe."

"Thank you." He seemed on the verge of saying something else, but then he rapped on the carriage top. The driver snapped the reins, and the matched bays took off at a brisk walk. Elizabeth watched until the back of the carriage disappeared from sight, but her husband did not look back.

Restless nights led into bleak days. Elizabeth managed to leave her rooms only to make her tenant visits, and that only because she could not bear to disappoint anyone else. She picked at the food Lucy brought her, more to satisfy Lucy than out of hunger.

One night, when sleep was even more elusive than usual and her mind refused to stop presenting her with lists of her faults, she found her way to the cupboard of remedies in the still room. The bottle of laudanum she had grown familiar with during the days of her husband's illness was there, promising a few hours of oblivion. She took the bottle from the shelf, its weight heavier in her hand than she remembered. Mrs. Reynolds must have refilled it.

There was enough to purchase her more than a night's sleep if she were not mistaken. Would that not be the simplest solution for everyone? Darcy could be spared the bitter reminder of her presence. He could marry again. He would have no difficulty finding a new bride, one who could be a real wife to him and a better sister to Georgiana. The idea of another woman in her place, lying in Darcy's arms at night, caused her eyes to swim with tears, but she wanted him to find the happiness he deserved. She knew it would never be with her.

It would be no loss to her family; she was already lost to them. If anyone were to miss her at all, it would be a few of the tenants who had come to depend upon her visits and perhaps Pandora. But Pandora would be sold to a new mistress; she would not pine.

She heard footsteps echoing in the empty hallways and quickly put the bottle away, fearing her thoughts would be evident. It was only a chambermaid carrying a pile of linens, but she turned curiously at the sight of her mistress. Elizabeth closed the cupboard and slowly made her way down the hall to her rooms. It would have to wait until tomorrow night. She did not want any more scandal to touch Darcy, so no one must suspect what she was about. Mrs. Reynolds would guess when she found the laudanum bottle empty, but she would keep the secret out of loyalty to the family.

Oddly, Elizabeth felt lighter than she had before and was able to drift off to sleep quickly.

When she awoke, her mind remained clear as to what she must do. It was easier to view the future when it was only a day long. She thought she might even take a walk around the grounds after her tenant visits. She would need to be sure all their needs were met today, since it would be her last chance.

Lucy appeared with her accustomed tray of breakfast. Elizabeth waved it aside as usual; but Lucy, with a tenacity quite unlike her, shook her head. "Madam, you must eat."

"Thank you for your concern, Lucy. I am not hungry at the moment, but I will eat something later."

"No, madam, you *must eat*."

"Not now, Lucy." Elizabeth spoke more sharply than was her wont.

Red flags appeared in the girl's cheeks, but she stood her ground. "Madam, if you do not eat, I... I will tell Mrs. Reynolds."

Elizabeth almost laughed at what was clearly the worst threat Lucy could imagine. "Lucy..."

"Mrs. Darcy, you have not had your courses these three months. You must eat."

For a moment Elizabeth could not understand what she was speaking of. Surely it had not been so long. She cast her mind back but could not produce details. How often had her courses come since she had been at Pemberley? Was it only the once? It must have been, and she had been too preoccupied to notice.

This could not be happening. How could she raise a child when her husband barely spoke to her? And what of her own plans? Suddenly, the decision was no longer wholly her own.

As if from a great distance, she heard herself say, "Yes, of course, Lucy. I promise you, I will eat."

Looking mollified but distrustful, Lucy set the tray on the bedside table and poured out the tea. Clearly she did not intend to leave until her mistress had eaten. Elizabeth took a muffin and raised it to her mouth. It seemed tasteless, as everything did these days, but she forced herself through the motions of chewing and swallowing. She washed down the dryness with a swallow of bitter tea. Seeing Lucy's eyes still upon her, she took another bite then dropped the remains on the delicate porcelain plate.

"Now the bread and jam, madam."

When had Lucy become so intransigent? Elizabeth sighed, then obediently spread the jam on the bread. The sweetness made it a little more palatable, so she finished it, then pushed the tray away. "Please, Lucy, no more."

"Very well, madam. A little at a time. I know how ill you have been, and it should pass soon; but you must keep up your strength."

Elizabeth looked at her in confusion, then realised what she meant. Lucy thought she had kept to her rooms because of her condition. It was almost amusing. No doubt it was better to let her think that than to admit to her despair, especially if she might be carrying the heir to Pemberley.

She could not keep back the tears. Covering her eyes, she managed to say, "That will be all, Lucy."

Chapter 14

WHEN A FOOTMAN BROUGHT her a letter a week later, Elizabeth's first impulse was to tell him to take it away. The post had brought her nothing but pain, and she saw no reason why that would change. But that would not be suitable for the mistress of Pemberley, so she accepted the letter. The direction was in the firm handwriting she remembered from the letter Darcy sent her when they were engaged, but this would not be a love note. She wished she had appreciated more the one he had written her then.

She was half afraid to break the seal, not knowing what instructions he might have for her. She reminded herself he was neither unfair nor unkind, and whatever he had written, it could be no worse than what he had already said to her. Still, she retreated to her bedroom to read it.

Madam,
We have made substantial progress in our efforts here. Your sister has been recovered and is presently at your uncle's

house in Cheapside. Mr. Wickham has agreed to abide by his promise; their wedding is scheduled for next week. They will then travel into the north where he will take up a post in the regulars. I will remain in London for the ceremony and return to Pemberley at some point thereafter.

I hope this intelligence will provide you with some relief.

Fitzwilliam Darcy

Elizabeth's breath caught in her throat. It was so unexpected she hardly knew whether to believe it. He must have been in contact with her family. And with Wickham! She could scarcely credit it. She read the brief missive again, pausing at the indication that he would be attending the wedding. There was no reason he would participate in an event he must find repugnant unless he were somehow involved. Based on Wickham's earlier demands, she could only assume some money must have changed hands.

Was this why he had gone to London, to undertake this effort to bring about their marriage? She could not imagine how he would endure the mortification of it. She wanted—no, she longed to believe it was on her behalf. Two months ago, before their quarrel, it would have been. Now it was more likely he did it to minimise the scandal. Still, his letter indicated he must care about her state of mind at least to some degree. Otherwise, he need not have troubled himself to write. She reviewed the few lines again, searching for reason to hope.

Perhaps he regretted his harshness after his illness and wanted once more to establish a civil relationship. The sheer relief that she might not have to live with his enmity made her stomach lurch in a pleasant way, and she rested her hand over it. The baby. Perhaps that might please him, too. Perhaps it was not altogether hopeless.

She crossed to the desk to pen a carefully worded letter of thanks.

Elizabeth could not help but hope for a response to her letter, nor could she avoid feelings of discouragement when one did not come. But she was still determined to do her best to ensure a happier outcome than had seemed indicated prior to Darcy's departure. She thought of him often, of his generosity and virtues, and prayed that generosity would outweigh the resentful temper he had spoken of in the long ago days at Netherfield. She was by no means certain of it, but she continued her efforts to become the best mistress of Pemberley she could. This included spending more time with Georgiana and encouraging her confidence.

One day, as they sat together in the front drawing room, Georgiana spoke up with unusual determination. "Have you ever looked at the miniatures over the mantelpiece, Elizabeth?"

"Not closely." Elizabeth's needle moved nimbly through the fabric.

"Would you object if I removed one of them?"

Elizabeth set aside the handkerchief she was embroidering. She had been working earlier on a shirt for the baby Mrs. Tanner was expecting but found it drew her mind to the question of her own condition. Although she wished she could view the possibility of her own child with joy, she found it impossible to think of anything but how her husband would react to the news.

It was hard to forget that once she had produced the heir to Pemberley, there would be little inducement for Darcy to make their marriage more than in name only.

Yet still she longed for his presence and hoped he would be happy to see her on his return. It was desperately confusing.

She disentangled herself from her bleak thoughts to focus on Georgiana. "I cannot see why you should not if you so desire. Would you show me which one you have in mind?"

"If you wish to see it, which I doubt that you do."

Now curious, Elizabeth approached the fireplace. She had never examined this particular group in detail. Her eyes lingered on a miniature of Darcy, clearly taken some years ago, but with a familiar smile on his face. She recognised Lady Catherine de Bourgh and Colonel Fitzwilliam in two of the others. There was one of Mr. Darcy as a boy and one in a matching frame of another child she did not recognise but with the Darcy family looks. Then her eyes alighted on an unexpected face. What was Mr. Wickham doing in this family collection? It must be the doing of old Mr. Darcy. She could not imagine her husband making such a choice.

"No, I have no objection whatsoever to removing it." Elizabeth felt no need to ask which miniature Georgiana meant. "I agree it has no place there."

Georgiana's shoulders relaxed. "No, it does not. I will ask Mrs. Reynolds to put it in storage and to rearrange the others."

Elizabeth pointed to the miniature of the unknown child. "I do not recognise this boy. Who is he?"

"That one? Next to Fitzwilliam? That is Thomas."

"Thomas?" Perhaps it was a cousin she had not heard of.

"My brother. It is the only likeness of him that was taken."

Her brother? How had Elizabeth remained unaware of this piece of Darcy family history? Thomas looked to be nine or ten years old in the portrait, and the matching one of her husband suggested they were close in age. "I had not realised you had another brother."

Georgiana's surprise was evident in her expression. "Yes, though I do not remember him well. I was still a child when he died, and he was much older than I. Fitzwilliam could tell you more about him."

Elizabeth did not doubt this was true, but if he had not mentioned him in their months of marriage, it seemed unlikely he would now. "What happened to him?"

"Smallpox. Both Thomas and my mother succumbed to it. My father had it as well. He recovered, although he was scarred by it."

It must have been a terrible time for Darcy. She suddenly remembered something he had said once—*I fear losing the people I care for.* "But you and Fitzwilliam were spared?"

"Fitzwilliam was safe at Cambridge. I never became ill."

"How dreadful for all of you." She wondered what it had been like for Darcy to return home to a decimated family.

Georgiana shrugged. "It was a long time ago."

"Thank you for telling me." Elizabeth had many more questions, but she suspected this conversation was more upsetting to Georgiana than it appeared.

Georgiana looked puzzled and seemed about to say something, but then she fell silent and returned to her book.

※

The day was unseasonably warm, and Elizabeth was tired by the time she returned from a walk through the Pemberley grounds. No sooner had she entered the doors of Pemberley than one of the maids gave her the welcome news that Mr. Darcy had returned.

"Where is he?" A surge of gladness filled Elizabeth's heart.

"In his study, madam."

Elizabeth hesitated. The proper behaviour would be to return to her room to refresh herself before seeing her husband, but she had missed him too much and wondered too long about this reunion. She hurried down the hallway to the study.

The door was open, though he was alone, seated behind his desk. He looked healthier than he had when he left, still a little thin, but with good colour and a general air of strength about him. It warmed her just to see him.

He did not seem to notice her until she said, "Welcome home."

He looked up then rose to his feet formally. "Thank you."

"You were much missed." She smiled at him, feeling a little shy.

"I appreciate the sentiment, Elizabeth, but it was not your gratitude I was seeking." He resumed his seat and lifted a glass of brandy to his lips.

"It is not gratitude that makes me glad to see you." Even as she said the words, she knew they were pointless. His unsmiling visage told her that much. Her dreams that his actions in London represented continuing affection for her were just that: dreams. He was polite, nothing more. But she would not give up so easily and go back to their long silences. "Tell me, how was your trip?"

"Uneventful. I assume you would like to hear about your sister Lydia."

Heat rose in her cheeks. Was he reminding her of her disgraceful connections? "No, in fact, I would prefer to hear about you."

"You are not concerned for your sister?"

Perhaps she had hoped for too much in thinking he would be polite. She raised her chin. "You have already told me she is alive, married, and to live far away. Since the past cannot be undone, that is the best I can hope for, so there is nothing further you can say to reassure me."

He took a swallow of brandy. "Do you not wish to know whether she was party to Mr. Wickham's plans?"

She had not considered that possibility. Lydia, although vain and frivolous, had never possessed a talent for mischief making. But if Lydia had known what Wickham was planning, it would be a disgrace Darcy would never be able to forgive. "I suppose I ought."

"She was not. She was unaware of the contents of the letter beyond her own note."

"That is, I suppose, a relief. I would rather her worst fault be silliness than larceny."

Colonel Fitzwilliam appeared in the doorway. "Darcy, have you... Pardon me, Mrs. Darcy; I had not realised you were here. I hope you are well?"

Her husband had not cared to ask that question. "I am, I thank you."

"I will not interrupt you further then." He bowed, as if to depart.

Suddenly, her hurt turned to a form of anger that her husband did not even show her that much courtesy. "There is no need. I was merely expressing my *gratitude* to Mr. Darcy, and we have quite exhausted the subject. I shall see you at supper, I presume?"

The colonel gave her a puzzled look. "Of course. I shall look forward to it."

She moved past him, hoping she could keep her countenance until she was out of sight.

Her first impulse was to flee to her room and to lick the wounds of her lost hopes, but she was tired of hiding in her rooms, tired of crying, and tired of feeling unloved. Instead, she made her way to the kitchen and asked the cooks to put together a basket of food for the Tanners.

Delivering it calmed her a little. The children's pleasure in her visit lifted her spirits, and seeing the fading bruises on Mrs. Tanner's face reminded Elizabeth of how much she still had to be thankful for in her husband. Even if he never cared for her again, at least he did not misuse his position.

She delayed her return to the house as long as possible, arriving back just in time for supper. She ate it in silence, letting Darcy, Georgiana, and Colonel Fitzwilliam carry the conversation. It seemed the wisest course, since she felt unable to discern what Darcy wanted from her. Did he wish for her to be animated or to try to be invisible? To act as mistress of Pemberley or not to interfere with his household? Or did he wish her to leave completely?

The situation was untenable, but she could not imagine discussing it with her husband after the debacle of their first conversation. Finally, when she retired after supper complaining of a headache, she decided to take pen to paper. At least this way she would not have to witness his reaction to her questions.

She wrote two drafts before she was satisfied her words were neutral enough, then recopied it yet again after tears stained her fair copy. She crumpled the early drafts and tossed them on the fire; it would not do for Lucy or one of the chambermaids to find them. She read through the final version one last time.

Although you said you did not want my gratitude, you have it in any case as well as my deep appreciation that you would take on the burden and mortification to help my poor sister. It was an act of charity on your part, by no means deserved by the recipients, but you have my heartfelt thanks as well as my regret and apologies to have ever brought this situation upon you.

It was not my gratitude which caused me to be glad to see you today any more than it was gratitude that made me pray desperately for you when you were missing or that kept me by your bedside during your illness, at least until such a time as you made your wishes for my absence known. I understand fully that my late-blooming affection and admiration are unwelcome to you. I cannot say I deserve anything more after my poor judgement and unkind behaviour.

My purpose in writing to you is to request direction as to how I may least impinge upon your peace of mind given our awkward circumstances. I have misjudged your desires in the past and have no wish to do so again, nor to force my company on you. Therefore, I would ask your guidance as to the extent to which you wish me to participate in your house-hold or even if you would prefer me to absent myself from Pemberley. My only wish is for your comfort and happiness, and you may be assured I will follow your instructions in every particular.

I will await your direction. If it is of importance to you in coming to a decision, it is my belief that I am presently with child.

You need not be alarmed that I will make a habit of forcing my sentiments upon you, but on this one occasion, I will take the liberty to sign myself,

Your loving wife,

Elizabeth Darcy

It might be better to leave out the final part, but she feared she might never have another chance to tell him of her feelings. It would likely be unwelcome to him now, but perhaps some day, he might recall it with more fondness. Or perhaps that was no more than wishful thinking.

She folded the letter carefully and dripped hot wax to form a seal, blowing across it to cool it more quickly. If he received it tonight, it would be that much less time before she had an answer and an end to this terrible uncertainty.

She was in luck; Darcy had not yet retired, so she was able to give the letter to Ferguson with instructions to deliver it personally to her husband when he came upstairs. Now all she could do was wait. She doubted she would sleep tonight, so she settled herself in the window seat, a book beside her which she could pretend to be reading if Lucy reappeared.

Hours later, the candle long since burnt out, Elizabeth started when a peremptory knock sounded at the adjoining door. Without waiting for an invitation, Darcy opened the door and strode in. He stopped in the middle of the room as if allowing his eyes to adjust to the darkness. Her letter was in his hand.

His countenance bespoke disturbance, if not anger. He approached her as she sat in the window seat, holding her letter as if it were a weapon. "What means this, madam?"

She looked up at him, tracing his features with her eyes. If only she had recognised her feelings for him earlier, she might have been allowed to caress them with her fingers, to feel the warmth of his skin. But it was not to be. "Exactly what it says."

"Do you wish to establish yourself elsewhere?"

She dropped her eyes. So it was to be exile from him. "If that is what you wish."

He placed one booted foot on the window seat, leaning closer to her. "I *asked* what *you* wish."

She leaned her head back against the carved wood. "If all else is equal, I would prefer to remain here."

"And you are with child?" There was no warmth in his tone.

"I believe so. I am not yet certain."

He spun away and crossed to the bed, throwing the letter upon it. "Elizabeth, I will not mistreat you or indeed treat you with less than respect. You need do nothing to please me in order to earn that. I pray you, in future, do not torment me by pretending to sentiments you do not possess. I would rather have your honest dislike."

"There was no pretence in my letter. I would never lie about my affection for someone."

"Indeed? It seems to me you did little else during the first months of our marriage." There was a world of bitterness in his voice.

She pressed her fingertips against the cool glass. They would leave a mark that would have to be cleaned in the morning. "I did not lie to you about my feelings. I chose not to contradict your assumptions. There is a difference."

"To you, perhaps. Whether you deceived me or whether you allowed me to deceive myself does not change the outcome for me. Good night, madam."

"Wait!" She rose to her feet and caught his arm. As he turned back to look at her, she caught a hint of a haunted look in his eyes. She could not resist the urge to tuck back his stray lock of hair and let her fingers rest afterwards on his cheek. It had been so long since she had touched him. "Fitzwilliam, I will not quarrel with you. It was unconscionable of me to deceive you, but I could find no other option. I will not deceive you now."

"You cannot change your feelings as you would your gloves. Please, Elizabeth." It was as if he were torn between staying and departing.

"If there is one thing of which you cannot accuse me, sir, it is of learning to love you too quickly." She caressed the line of his jaw.

Her teasing tone must have gone amiss, because his countenance turned grim again. "Do not speak to me of love, Elizabeth. If you no longer hold the past against me, I am satisfied. No more is needed."

"So you do not believe me when I speak of caring."

He crossed his arms. "No, madam, I do not."

She could find no warmth in him now, no sign of love, no trace of desire, even though they were alone in her room and she wore nothing but a summer nightgown. Apparently, he had lost interest in that aspect of her as well.

She knew then that nothing she could say would convince him, perhaps because he did not trust her or perhaps because he did not want her love. She looked into his implacably distant eyes. So, it was beyond repair. All she could do was learn to live with a love that would never be returned and the knowledge of the opportunity she had lost. Perhaps someday it would no longer hurt as it did now.

"Then I will not trouble you with sentiments you do not wish to hear." She tried to speak lightly, but her voice began to shake. Choosing retreat over a rout, she returned to the window seat where she had an excuse to look away from him.

The sound of the door opening and closing again told her he had departed. Exhausted, she lowered her face into her arms and wept.

What Darcy needed was a gallop over the countryside, but unfortunately, that would have to wait until morning. Not that first light was far off; he had stayed downstairs until quite late, since he did not wish to think long before he fell asleep, not with Elizabeth in bed just beyond the sitting room. Instead, he had found her letter and confronted her, and now he prowled his room like a wounded tiger, full of rage and helplessness.

He tried to find excuses for her behaviour. Women with child were often moody and prone to strange reasoning, were they not? He should not have spoken so coldly to her on his return, but he could not bear the happiness on her face when she saw him, knowing it was not for him. Perhaps she had sought to please him by that incomprehensible letter, not realising how much more it would hurt him to raise his hopes again.

But was it possible she meant what she had said? He quashed the voice inside which wanted to believe her. There was no point in even considering it. His goal was a civil friendship which would allow them both to survive this mockery of a marriage. Tonight that objective seemed a distant one.

What had she said? That she had worried about him when he was ill? When he had finally awoken from his illness, she was nowhere to be found. Hardly the action of a devoted wife. Certainly there had been fever dreams where she had been present, placing cool cloths on his forehead and holding his hand, but that had been wishful thinking. The doubting voice spoke up again. If only he could shut his ears to it!

Ferguson emerged from the dressing room with Darcy's nightshirt and gown. The valet moved silently and efficiently as he performed the nightly rituals, turning down the bed and hanging up the topcoat and waistcoat Darcy had abandoned over the back of a chair. Darcy stopped pacing long enough to allow Ferguson to remove his boots, but his thoughts would not stop.

"Ferguson?"

"Yes, sir?"

"When I was ill, did Mrs. Darcy attend to me?" Here would be his proof to quiet the inner voice. Darcy stripped off his shirt and handed it to Ferguson.

"Quite constantly, sir. She was here day and night while you were the most ill. She was a most devoted nurse." Ferguson folded the shirt with the utmost care. "Until you told her to leave, that is, sir."

Darcy rounded on his valet with a temper not often shown to his servants. "I never told her to leave."

"As you say, sir." Ferguson disappeared with the shirt and boots into the dressing room.

No. It made no sense. Darcy strode to the dressing room. "What do you mean I told her to leave? Did she tell you that?"

"No, sir; I was present on the occasion. It was the day your fever broke." Ferguson knelt and began polishing one of Darcy's boots with a soft cloth, as if there were nothing unusual about this conversation, as if nothing depended on it.

Darcy gritted his teeth. "What did I say?"

"I cannot recall your exact words, but it was to the effect that you wished her gone and wanted nothing further to do with her and that she should trouble you no more. You did not seem confused at the time. No doubt it is an effect of the laudanum that you do not recall it."

"Damned laudanum. Never let them give it to me again." Darcy gripped the doorframe until his hand hurt. "What did Mrs. Darcy do?"

"I am sure I could not say." Ferguson busied himself checking the gleam of the leather then switched to the second boot.

"Ferguson, I am damned sure you *can* say and that you have been eagerly anticipating the opportunity to do so. Tell me *now*."

"As you wish, sir. I believe she wept a little and asked if you meant it; then, on your affirmation, she left. She did not return for several days, although she instructed me to inform her as to your condition every few hours. She mostly kept to her rooms, except when she was visiting tenants."

"*Visiting tenants!?*"

"Yes, sir."

Damn Ferguson and his attempts to manage him. Darcy went to his desk and hunted for Elizabeth's letter, then remembered he had left it in her room. Damn the letter, too. He needed to know exactly what it said.

Elizabeth awoke to a sensation of movement and warmth. "What is it?" she murmured, still half-asleep.

"Shh, Elizabeth. You fell asleep in the window seat, and I am taking you to your bed." It sounded like Darcy's voice, but it could not be, for it was gentle and calm. Perhaps it was a dream, with the warmth of his arms supporting her and her head resting on his shoulder, but it was a sweet dream.

The warmth disappeared, replaced by the coolness of the bedsheets. She opened her eyes to see her husband, clad only in his nightshirt, leaning over her. "Fitzwilliam? What brings you here?"

"Go back to sleep. We can talk in the morning." He bent down to kiss her lightly.

She might be dreaming, but she did not want him to leave, not when he was being kind to her. She wrapped her arms around his neck, drawing him closer to kiss him once more. He seemed willing to cooperate, his lips meeting hers slowly and gently. The contact was such a comfort that her arms tightened around him, and he responded by teasing her lips apart for the deep, disturbingly pleasant kisses she remembered so well.

It was several minutes before he disentangled himself, and by that time he was breathing heavily. "Elizabeth, I am only human. You are half-asleep and know not what you do."

She would not dream his withdrawal. Elizabeth shook her head to drive off the last vestiges of sleep. "I assure you, sir, I am quite awake. Was there something you wanted?"

His mouth twisted and he took a moment before answering. "I came to apologise to you, both for my anger and for something I apparently said while under the influence of laudanum. It always makes me see things that are not there and confuses me as to what is real. That is why I detest it so."

It felt like an odd reversal of his illness; this time, she was the one lying in bed while he sat on the edge beside her. "I am not certain of your meaning, sir."

"Ferguson tells me I sent you away. I assure you, had I been in my right mind, I would never have done so."

"Oh." She wondered whether he meant he would not have thought it or would have been too polite to say it. "I hope my presence was not disturbing to you."

"Not at all. Ferguson tells me you were a devoted nurse."

He was not making it easy for her to follow her promise to keep her feelings about him to herself. "I was worried about you."

He brushed her cheek with the back of his fingers. "Thank you."

Was there tenderness in his eyes, or was she only seeing what she wished to see? Shakily, she said, "I am glad you are well again and home safe."

He hesitated. "And you are with child?"

Her lips turned up with amusement. "My answer to that has not changed since the last time you asked me it."

"Sometimes I am a slow learner." Slowly, as if he expected her to stop him, he placed his hand on the swell of her waist.

Though his fingers but rested there, the heat of his touch ran deep within her. Her lips tingled. "There has not been much change as yet."

"Not much, but perhaps a greater fullness." His consideration of her body was oddly intimate. His eyes swung to meet hers, then, with a fluid motion, he bent down to kiss her again. His lips lingered only briefly, then he sat up again. "Sleep well, Elizabeth."

"Good night," she whispered to his retreating back.

Chapter 15

LUCY HAD ALREADY REMINDED Elizabeth twice that morning to eat her breakfast, but her efforts were in vain. This time Elizabeth's difficulties were not owing to distress. Rather, it was memories of the previous night that distracted her.

Darcy's behaviour mystified her. First quarrelsome and uninterested, then warm and apparently no longer indifferent. But even then he had made no attempt to stay with her, though he could not have thought she would object. The memory of his kiss made her lips tingle.

As difficult as she found it to ascertain her husband's thoughts, one thing seemed clear: he was as confused as she, though by what she could not guess. Even if part of him was angry with her, another part still maintained his attachment, it seemed. The question was what she should do about it.

She recalled the warmth of his arms around her. When they were first wed, it was an everyday occurrence. He had spent time with her then, tried to engage her interest in her new home, offered her parts of his life to share. It made her heartsick to think how little it had meant to her at the time and how much it would mean to her now! If only she had put aside her prejudices and allowed herself to see his good points sooner!

But regret for the past would not help. What she needed to remember now was that she had seen the old look in his eye again last night. If those feelings for her still existed in him, surely there must be something she could do to strengthen them. Hiding in her room was not the answer.

"Lucy, I believe I will have breakfast downstairs today."

"Yes, madam." Lucy gave her a distrusting look but picked up the tray and took it away.

Elizabeth searched through her jewelry box and found the necklace he had given her shortly after their quarrel. She fastened it around her neck, the cold metal of the pendant warming gradually against her skin. She would wear her blue dress, the one Darcy had liked so much. In the mirror, she tried out a teasing smile.

Yes. If it could be done, she would win his affections back.

⁂

For at least the tenth time, Darcy tore his thoughts away from what it had felt like to carry Elizabeth in his arms, her light summer nightgown failing to disguise the fact that she wore nothing under it. His steward was saying something, and again, he had missed it completely.

"You will see him, then?" Dunstan closed the account book and set it to one side.

"Of course." Darcy wondered what he had just agreed to.

Dunstan opened the study door and showed in one of the tenant farmers. "Mr. Smithson, sir."

Smithson. He tried to remember what he knew of the man but could conjure only a vague familiarity with the name.

The farmer's hands had clearly been washed especially for this momentous occasion, and a pretty girl perhaps a year or two younger than Georgiana accompanied him. Her eyes widened when she saw Darcy. What was it about him, Darcy wondered, that terrified women so? First Elizabeth, now this girl. Had he not done his best to be a generous and reasonable landlord?

Darcy motioned to the chairs opposite his desk. The girl perched on the edge of her chair as if ready to flee at any moment. "What can I do for you?"

The man's hands tightened on the brim of his hat. "Mr. Darcy, sir, we've summat of a problem. Young Tom Morrison, well, he *ought* to marry my daughter here, but he says he will not. Since he's one o' your labourers, sir, I hoped maybe you could help me."

The girl burst into tears.

Darcy sighed inwardly. He hated these cases. There was never a good resolution. He spoke directly to the girl. "Did he promise to marry you?"

She half-whispered something.

"I cannot hear you, child."

"Please, sir, is Mrs. Darcy here?" she asked shakily.

What in God's name did Elizabeth have to do with this? Darcy gave Dunstan a questioning look. The steward leaned down and said in his ear, "Mrs. Darcy has been hearing cases while you were away and earlier, during your illness. Perhaps the girl did not realise you were back."

Interesting. And no one had seen fit to mention it to him. No doubt they thought Elizabeth would have told him. As if she were likely to tell him anything! Though that morning at breakfast, she had been quite animated, so perhaps she might have told him had she the opportunity. "Does Mrs. Darcy know anything of this case?"

"Not to my knowledge, sir." Dunstan stepped back.

Darcy drummed his fingers on his desk. So the girl wanted Elizabeth sitting in judgement rather than him. After all his years as master of Pemberley, this young thing had the audacity to want Elizabeth instead. "Once again, did the young man promise to marry you?"

The girl, looking frankly terrified, opened her mouth as if to say something but no words came out. Her father pushed at her arm. "Tell Mr. Darcy."

This could go on for hours, and Darcy's patience had been eroded by his sleepless night. "Dunstan, would you be so kind as to ask Mrs. Darcy to attend me here?" Perhaps Elizabeth had some knowledge of the matter, and, he hoped, she would be pleased to be consulted.

Dunstan bowed and left the room. Darcy folded his hands on his desk, uncomfortable with the questions he needed to ask as well as his ignorance of what Elizabeth had done in his absence. He supposed he could not blame her for saying nothing. Their communications since his return had been strained at best. But she had kissed him as if she meant it.

He cleared his throat. "How long have you known Tom Morrison?"

Though he had addressed his question to the girl, her father again answered. "Mayhap half a year, sir."

Darcy was relieved to be interrupted by Elizabeth, who appeared in the doorway wearing a warm smile and that damned blue dress he always wanted to tear off her.

"You asked for me, sir?"

He rose to his feet. "Yes, Mrs. Darcy. We have a family here seeking redress, and the young lady involved seems disappointed to be facing my judgement rather than yours; so I thought to invite you to join us."

There it was again, that damned flash of fear, as if she expected him to beat her. At least she covered it quickly this time. "As you wish, Mr. Darcy."

He indicated the girl with a tilt of his head. "Perhaps she will be more inclined to answer your questions than mine. We are attempting to determine a young man's intentions towards her."

A line appeared on Elizabeth's brow. She moved to sit by the girl's side. "Sylvia, is it not?" The girl nodded, wiping her eyes on her sleeve.

How had Elizabeth known her name when he had not?

"Is your baby brother well? And your mother?"

"Very well, Mrs. Darcy." Sylvia's voice still shook.

"I am glad to hear it. Now, Sylvia, although we are not really acquainted, you and I, perhaps you can tell me what this is about."

Darcy could not help but admire the gentle persuasion Elizabeth was bringing to bear.

"It was Tom Morrison. He... he..." She leaned towards Elizabeth and said something too quietly for Darcy to hear.

Elizabeth's lips tightened. She whispered back to the girl but was answered only with tears. Darcy sat back, curious to see what she would make of the situation.

The man spoke up. "He refuses to marry her, ma'am, and there is a babe coming, so they *must* be wed."

Elizabeth's eyes met Darcy's uncertainly. He said, "Well, Mrs. Darcy, we await your judgement."

She looked at him intently for a moment more then turned back to Sylvia, handing her a handkerchief. "Do you wish to marry him, Sylvia?"

The girl shook her head vehemently.

Her father raised a hand as if to cuff her, then apparently remembered where he was. "You must marry him. No other man'll ever have you now."

The colour drained from Sylvia's face, but Elizabeth appeared to ignore him completely. "How old are you, child?"

"Almost fifteen, ma'am."

"Did you consent to what he did to you?"

There was a long silence. "No, ma'am."

Her father spoke to Darcy. "It makes no difference, Mr. Darcy. She must marry him."

Darcy crossed his arms over his chest. Now he was grateful for the whim that had caused him to turn this case over to Elizabeth. He did not want to be the one to force the girl into an unwanted marriage with a man of that sort.

Elizabeth's cheeks were bright with colour. "You realise what it will mean if you do not marry him?"

"I don't care, ma'am. He's a brute. I'd as soon starve in the streets."

Elizabeth folded her hands and turned to Darcy. "There seems to be no possibility of making everyone happy in this case, but this is my suggestion. I will ask Mrs. Reynolds to find Sylvia a position in the household here. Her baby can stay with her own mother or be fostered out. If Sylvia serves us well until she is of age and then finds a man she wishes to wed, I will give her a dowry suitable to compensate for her past. Dunstan?"

"Fifty pounds would be adequate, madam," the steward said.

Sylvia burst into tears again and grabbed at Elizabeth's hand, holding it to her lips.

Darcy addressed Sylvia's father. "Will this be acceptable to you?"

"I suppose, sir." He did not look pleased.

"Dunstan, look into the situation with Tom Morrison. If you find any cause for concern, dismiss him and tell him not to set foot here again."

"Yes, sir," Dunstan said.

Even then it was not simple. Sylvia, fear evident in her face, clung to Elizabeth when her father tried to take her away. Elizabeth rang for a maid to take her to the kitchens until she could speak with Mrs. Reynolds.

When they were finally gone, Elizabeth said, "I wonder what she thought would happen if she went home with him? Well, no matter. They can no doubt put her to work in the kitchens until we come up with something more satisfactory."

"You will have a devoted servant for life, Elizabeth."

"I hope you do not object to my decision."

"Not in the least. It will not cost much more than it would have to bring the marriage about, and the girl will be far happier."

He gestured to Dunstan to leave, but before he could, Elizabeth said, "Mr. Dunstan, could you set aside the dowry money from my funds now?"

"Certainly, madam."

"There is no need for it to come from your pin money, Elizabeth. It can come from the general estate funds."

Dunstan cleared his throat. "Mrs. Darcy pays for all her charity work from her own money, sir. I have explained to her that it is not necessary, but she prefers it so."

Darcy raised his eyebrows and looked over at Elizabeth, who seemed to have found something intensely interesting outside the window. "Henceforth, please take the money from the general account."

Elizabeth turned to him, a teasing smile hovering about her lips. "Perhaps, sir, you might wish to examine my expenditures before you make such rash statements."

Dunstan took a step forward and reached for an account book, but Darcy waved him back. "There is no need. Spend what you wish, Elizabeth. It will not bankrupt me."

Her smile grew wider. "Or at least Mr. Dunstan will warn you before it reaches that point."

"No doubt." At least Elizabeth looked happier than she had prior to his accident. Perhaps his absence had given her time to adjust to her situation here without the strain of his presence. He would not think about the way she had kissed him the night before. He would not. "Your judgement was a good one."

"Thank you. I am glad it meets with your approval. I confess, I had not thought to have any involvement in these matters now that you have returned."

"Do you object to it?" It would be just his luck that what he intended as a statement of confidence in her instead should be a burden.

"Not at all. I enjoy being aware of what is happening on the estate. Mr. Dunstan has been kind enough to educate me somewhat in that regard during your absence."

A stab of jealousy hit him. She had never cared to ask him about the estate. Did she prefer Dunstan to him? Was he the reason for her good cheer? He swallowed the bile in his throat, reminding himself of Dunstan's loyalty to him. "I take it you knew something of the circumstances."

"In fact, no. I have met Sylvia when calling on her mother, but that is all."

Here was his opening. "Someone mentioned yesterday that you have been making visits to the tenants."

Her eyes widened. "Yes, for some time. I thought you were aware of it, or I should have said something. Do you object?"

Damn it, why did she always assume he would object to everything she did? "Of course not. It is good of you to take the trouble. Perhaps at some point you would tell me about your visits."

"I would be happy to. Or, if you like, you are welcome to join me." She had moved next to his desk, so the light from the window was behind her, and he could make out the shape of her legs through the sheer blue fabric of that damnable dress.

"Perhaps I shall. When do you plan to go next?"

Again, the look of surprise. "Tomorrow morning if the weather is fair. But are you certain you are well enough?"

"I am quite well." Well enough to carry her warm, responsive body in his arms last night. No. He would not think about that.

"Then I should be delighted to have your company." She bent down and her lips brushed his cheek, the scent of rosewater drifting past him.

If he had turned his head, he could have caught her lips with his own, but he sat stock-still until the danger was passed. He was determined to take this slowly, to allow the new warmth she seemed to feel for him to grow before testing it with his demands. "Very well, madam."

Darcy arose early the following morning to avoid missing Elizabeth's departure. She had said nothing more about his accompanying her after their conversation the previous day, so he was uncertain if she would wait for him. But she had been, to all external evidence, in good cheer, and she had chosen to sit beside him after dinner as they listened to Georgiana play.

At least last night had been less of a torment for him than the one before. The knowledge that Elizabeth would not turn him away if he went to her no longer tortured him after her judgement about Sylvia. Once he had the opportunity to think it through, he had realised why she had leapt so quickly to the girl's defence. She knew what it meant to pay the price Sylvia had paid, and it was because of him. The very thought that Elizabeth might feel that pain and distress with him was enough to keep temptation in check. For now, he would have to settle for the knowledge that her dislike of him seemed to be waning, and she did not find it unpleasant to kiss him. Perhaps, if he did not impose himself upon her, the seed of warmth she seemed to feel for him might have the chance to flourish. Perhaps. It was a word he was coming to detest.

Darcy reined in the horses and brought the phaeton to a stop, but before he could step out, Elizabeth's warm hand descended upon his arm. She put a finger to her lips, then rummaged in the basket until she found several twists of paper. Without a by-your-leave she slipped them in the pocket of his topcoat. Darcy could feel the pressure of her hand against his hip. Was she deliberately trying to drive him mad or had she no idea?

He circled the phaeton and offered her his hand. The bewitching smile she gave him as she stepped down left him barely able to think clearly, but he took the basket from her and followed her down the rough path to the cottage.

When Elizabeth knocked at the door, he could hear cries of "Mrs. Darcy!" and scurrying footsteps inside. The door eventually opened to reveal three small children fighting over the privilege of being first to greet their guest. Their spirited bickering stopped suddenly when he entered. The youngest of the children, a toddler, grabbed Elizabeth's skirt and tried to hide behind it.

A voice from the shadows at the back of the cabin said, "Children, say good day to Mr. Darcy."

"Good day, Mr. Darcy," the eldest two children chorused timidly, but the youngest hid his face again.

"Good day," he greeted them with equal civility.

Elizabeth handed the basket to the little girl, who lifted up the cloth to peek inside. A disappointed look came over her face, but she curtsied to Elizabeth and said, "Thank you kindly, Mrs. Darcy."

"They did not give me any sweets this morning in the kitchen," said Elizabeth with a sidelong glance at Darcy. "I am sorry, for I know how much you like them."

Darcy suddenly understood her meaning. "Let me see." He patted his pocket. "I am certain I have something..." He pulled out the twists of paper. "Would these be of interest?"

The little girl's face lit up. "Oh, thank you, Mr. Darcy!"

They were charming children, he decided. It was a pleasure to watch Elizabeth's playful manners with them. He wondered if she would be like that with their children as well and again returned to the damning question of what she felt about her condition. She showed more enthusiasm over choosing dinner menus than she did about the child she was expecting. Did she not want children? He could not believe that, having seen her pleasure in the tenant children. Did she simply not want *his* children? Was that why she had been so sympathetic to young Sylvia's predicament, because she knew all too well what it was like to carry the child of a man who had forced himself upon her?

Or was she disguising her feelings as she had in the past?

He watched as she crouched down to let the youngest child whisper something in her ear. It was one of the first things he had admired about her, the natural way she had with everyone. Everyone but him, it seemed.

He wished he could see into her mind to discover what lay behind her new warmth towards him, but he dared not ask. He had forced too much intimacy on her already in the course of their marriage, and now he needed to give her time if he wanted to earn her affection, to have her kiss him again the way she had two nights previously…

Or perhaps that was just a dream. After everything he had done, it would take a miracle to convince her to trust him, and miracles had been in short supply at Pemberley for many years.

Chapter 16

IT WAS MORE THAN an hour since Elizabeth had heard Darcy's footsteps going down the hall to his room—an hour of waiting, first with hope, then with increasing anxiety, to see if he would come to her tonight. They had been in accord so much more these last two days, and it seemed as if he had enjoyed her presence. He even sought it out to some extent, joining her on her tenant visits and then later asking her to ride with him. But he stayed in his own room tonight, as he had ever since their quarrel.

She tried to silence the voice within her that suggested he might have lost interest in sharing her bed. She could not believe that, given his kiss two nights ago. Perhaps it was not an urgent desire, but it was there. The difficulty must be something else.

Perhaps he was concerned about his reception if he appeared in her bedroom. It did not make sense, since she had made every attempt to show him he would be welcome, but she was beginning to understand he was sometimes less certain of himself than he appeared.

Apparently, she would have no answer tonight. It was a disappointment; she wanted to be his wife, not an acquaintance living in the same house, and this was the strongest assertion of that. Or would be, if he would only come to her again.

She missed the sensation of his arms around her. Would she feel it once more?

She smoothed the fine silk nightdress her aunt Gardiner had given her as a wedding present. She had never worn it before, choosing instead simple shifts. She had been too embarrassed by its translucent fabric and low-cut neckline in the early days of her marriage, and then there had been no reason to wear it afterwards. It had been her hope that tonight it would be an indication to Darcy that she welcomed his presence.

But what if he required more than welcome? He had been hurt badly by their quarrel, of that she had no doubt, now that she had experienced what such rejection meant. Perhaps he needed more reassurance that she would not again throw harsh words at him.

There was a way to test it if she dared. In a moment of desperate resolution, she took up the matching silk dressing gown and wrapped it around herself. A last look in the mirror showed she was as ready as she would ever be. She rinsed her damp palms in a basin of cool water, then dried them on the embroidered towel.

It seemed a long distance across the sitting room which separated her bedroom from her husband's, but at the same time, it was too soon when she reached his door. But she would not back down now. She forced herself to knock.

"Yes?" Darcy's voice was barely muffled.

She opened the heavy door. She had spent so much time in his room when he was ill, but now it was like a foreign country again.

"What brings you here, Elizabeth?" He was in his nightshirt, reclining on his bed. He laid down the book in his hand.

"The same thing that would bring any wife to her husband's bedchamber." She smiled in what she hoped was a winsome manner. She untied the sash of her dressing gown and slipped her arms out of the sleeves then laid it over the back of a chair. He could not possibly doubt her intention now.

"There is no need for this." His eyes travelled down her form and lingered for a moment before returning to her face. Apparently, her aunt's ideas of what would appeal to a gentleman were correct.

Emboldened, Elizabeth sat on the bed and laid her hand on his chest, feeling the warmth of him through the fabric of his nightshirt. "You do not come to me; therefore, I must come to you." She leaned forward to press her lips against his, but there was no answering response.

"Elizabeth, I will not have you sacrificing yourself for me."

Her smile faltered. This was not the response she wished for, but she had gone too far to stop now. She moved her hand, stroking him lightly from shoulder to waist, hoping he would not think her wanton. "It is no sacrifice."

He caught her hand and removed it from his body. "This is not what I want."

He was turning her away, although he was clearly tempted; his face showed not even a hint of warmth. Her gamble had failed, and now she was in worse straits than she had been before. She rose to her feet. "Then I shall trouble you no longer. Good night, sir."

Her cheeks burned as she made her way to the door. No, her entire body burned from shame. It was the second time her husband had dismissed her from his room, and it would be the last, for she could never brave this again. She almost looked back as she went through the door, but she did not think she could bear to discover he had gone back to his book.

She closed the door of her own bedchamber and leaned back against it. There would be no more efforts; she had thrown herself at him like a loose woman. If there was ever to be anything more to their marriage, it would have to come from him. But perhaps her behaviour tonight had disgusted him enough to remove that possibility.

With trembling fingers she unbuttoned the silk nightdress and let it fall to the floor, then kicked it into a corner. Tomorrow she would tell Lucy to dispose of it. She never wanted to see it again. She found one of her everyday plain linen shifts and pulled it over her head. The coarseness of it against her skin was a shock after the smooth silk, but she would grow accustomed to it again, just as she had grown accustomed to her empty bed.

So his respectful warmth to her during the day was nothing more than politeness. No, that was not true; she had seen the look of desire in his eyes, but apparently his distaste for her outweighed it. She threw herself down on the bed and buried her face in the pillow, her body shaking with silent sobs.

When she heard the door open, she did not raise her head. No doubt Lucy looking in and then realising her mistress should be left in privacy. It was not as if she could hide her tears; she was sure her eyes must be red and puffy. The click of the door closing again told her Lucy had left, and her tears began anew.

Then she felt a movement on the bed beside her and a hand on her shoulder. Lucy would never intrude so, and Elizabeth could not mistake that touch. She burrowed her face even deeper into the pillow. She could not even bring herself to care that he knew she was crying over him.

His hand massaged her shoulder. "Elizabeth, I am sorry to cause you such pain. More sorry than you can know."

It did not matter. His regrets could change nothing. She could not stop her tears.

"I know you came to me tonight out of the best of motives, and I appreciate that. The fault is mine."

The gentleness in his touch and his voice only made it worse. She gripped the bedsheets, wishing she could pull them over her and be hidden from his sight.

"Will you not look at me, Elizabeth?"

She shook her head. She did not ever want show him her face again. "You need explain nothing," she said into the pillow. "I understand perfectly. Had you wanted a loose woman to come to you, you would have paid for one."

She heard the hiss of indrawn breath. "I do not ever want to hear you speak that way again, Elizabeth. That is a gross untruth."

"I will speak as I wish." There was no point in anything else.

There was a silence which was interrupted only by the movement of his hand. "There is, I suppose, something to be said for that. I would rather hear the truth than what you think will best please me, just as I would rather you stayed away than come to me just to please me."

"It was not to please you. *That* is a hopeless task. Nothing I do pleases you." Sobs overtook her once more.

"That is not true. It pleases me to see you take an interest in the estate. It pleases me that you and Georgiana are better friends."

"Very well, it pleases you that I fulfill the expectations of the mistress of your household. Nothing more." She stopped speaking before her anger led her to say even more.

His hand stilled, but she could feel the heat of it through her nightdress. "It pleases me to see you smiling more often."

She struggled to control her breathing. There was no point in arguing, no point in noting that he did not mention being pleased to see *her*. He was being gentle and attentive. It was the best she could hope for, and she ought to appreciate it while it lasted. "Thank you." A deep breath in, a deep breath out.

"You need not thank me for the truth." His hand resumed its stroking. "It pleases me that you do not have a taste for mutton."

She could not believe she had heard correctly. She turned her head to look at him. "What has mutton to do with this?"

"I am not fond of it and am glad to see it appearing less often at dinner."

"Why did you not simply ask the cooks not to serve it?"

He moved her hair away from her eyes. "I suppose it was a habit. Mrs. Reynolds believes children should learn to eat what they are served without complaint."

"It has been a long time since you were a child." Despite the circumstances, she found it endearing.

"A very long time." His fingertips caressed her cheek, coming to rest on her lips.

A shock of heat ran through her. Her distress had kept her from wondering why he had come to her, but there could be only one reason. "I thought this was not what you wanted."

He looked off into the air. "I came here because I feared you had taken my words in a way I had not meant them, and it seems

I was correct." Then his eyes turned to watch her again. "And also because I could not forget how breathtaking you looked."

"Oh." She could make no sense of the conflicting urges inside her, both drawn to him and yet still hurt and angry.

He placed his hand over hers. "I would not wish you to do anything distasteful to yourself on my behalf." There was an odd note in his voice, almost of pleading.

She bit her lip. "You are not offended, then, by my behaviour?"

"Offended? Why should I be offended?" He sounded genuinely surprised at her words.

"It was at best indelicate and at worst ill-bred."

"To come to me?"

Heat burned her cheeks. "To express an interest in…" She could not find words.

"Elizabeth, if in any small part of yourself, be it the most minute corner of your soul, in truth wanted to be with me, I would be… beyond pleased."

"Then why did you send me away?"

He paused, as if trying to make a decision, then turned his face away from her. "The day I proposed to you, I kissed you out of selfish greed and desire, without a thought for what it would mean for you or a suspicion that you might object. Because of that, you lost your home and everything you loved. And I continued to take my pleasure in you, never considering how I might be hurting you. I knew I was not as successful as I hoped in bringing you to enjoyment of the act, but I thought with time and familiarity… but no matter." His dark eyes met hers. "If you think I have forgotten what my desires have cost you, if you think I do not remember what I have done to you every time I see you, you would be quite incorrect. That is why I seek to control my impulses with you and to assume any offer you make comes from a sense of duty rather than anything else."

There was no mistaking the pain in his voice. Elizabeth raised herself on her elbow and entwined her fingers with his. "Sir, you do yourself too much wrong."

"I doubt it."

"You were always gentle and considerate with me. I had no cause for complaint. If I felt any distress, it was out of my own… confusion." How could she explain it to him without confessing her own faults?

"Had no one, then, explained it to you?"

"No, I understood it well enough. It was not that." She could hardly believe they were discussing this. If it were not evident how important it was to him, she doubted she could force herself to speak. As it was, she could not bring herself to say what needed to be said. Finally, she sat up and blew out the candle on the bedside table. In the protective darkness, she leaned her head back against the headboard and closed her eyes. "I am well aware that ladies are supposed to feel nothing. That was not always my experience."

There was a heavy silence. "And that… troubled you?"

That was easier to answer. "I consider it a weakness. I thought you would take it as a sign of my ill-breeding."

"Good God, no! Far from it." His response was instant.

She let out a long breath of relief. So, that fear had been for naught. "Otherwise, it was not distressing at all, and I often found it comforting when you held me."

"Did you?" There was a catch in his voice.

She nodded, then, realising he could not see her, said, "Yes."

"Would you…" He hesitated. "Would you find it comforting if I held you now?"

Did he truly mean it? "Yes," she said, half-breath, half-sob.

"Then come." He led her by the hand through the darkness to the sitting room door, then across the sitting room and into his bedroom. Not to his bed though. Instead, he paused, turning to cup her face in his hands. He did not say anything, just looked into her eyes as if trying to solve a puzzle. His thumbs caressed the corners of her jaw, and she felt her mouth grow dry and her lips tingled.

She expected him to kiss her, but instead, he drew her head against his shoulder. The warmth of him and his tenderness as he held her sent a shuddering sigh through her. She pressed her hands against his back, holding him tightly, the way she had wanted to when he was injured. The fabric of his nightshirt rubbed against her cheek, and she closed her eyes to appreciate the happiness she felt in his arms.

It was not long before she became aware of the tension in his body, the pressure of his arousal hard against her. It sent a new awareness through her, one that seemed to touch her every limb, and she became acutely aware of the weight of her shift against her breasts. A tightness between her legs begged for relief.

Yet Darcy did nothing, although she was almost certain he wished to. Perhaps if she initiated it—but no, that had not worked well earlier. But then, he had come to her. She tilted her head to see his face, hoping for a clue there, only to discover his eyes fixed on her.

One of them would have to do something if it were not always to remain thus. Elizabeth touched the tip of her tongue to her dry lips. No, from the look on his face, there was no mistaking what he wanted, and that very look was bringing forth more desire in her. But she dared not act, not when he had refused her kiss in this very room not more than half an hour past.

Still, she could indicate receptivity. She tipped her chin up, moving her face closer to his until she could feel the warmth of his breath tickling her cheek. Then his mouth was against hers, not gently as she expected but with urgent hunger that made her gasp.

Instinctively, she knew how to meet the raw need in him, arching herself against him and gripping his shoulders. A guttural sound burst forth from his throat as his hands strained to pull her ever closer. So he *did* still want her. Intoxicated by the knowledge, she ran her hands down his back.

Finally, he broke away, his breathing uneven. "Are you certain this is what you want?"

"Quite certain." And suddenly she *was* certain, not just to be close to him or to please him but with a sense that she needed his touch.

Then, her feet left the floor as he swung her up into his arms, carrying her the last few steps to his bed. But he did not put her down, instead looking intensely at her. "I want to learn what brings you pleasure."

She buried her face in his shoulder, her cheeks burning. "Do not ask me to say. I am too embarrassed already."

"Then I must discover it for myself." He lowered her to the bed. His hand curved around her breast as he lay beside her, his thumb skimming across the sensitive tip. His voice took on a new roughness. "And discover it I shall, so do not attempt to hide it from me. Do you understand?"

She nodded, acutely aware of his hand, wanting him to touch her that way again. When at last he did and a shaft of pleasure rushed through her, she raised her eyes to his. "I will try not to hide it." But she could hear a trembling in her voice.

"In fact," he said in an autocratic tone she had not heard in some time, "I do not wish anything to be hidden." He tugged at the ties of her nightdress. "Nothing at all."

Her eyes widened. He had never asked this of her in the past, though she had heard of men who liked their women unclothed. Her skin burned at the idea of him looking at her so. But she would not deny him, although the very thought sent tension spiralling through her. She sat up and drew the shift over her head then let it fall to the floor. She could not look at him, but she could feel his eyes on her body.

His hands cupped her breasts, and then he rested his forehead against them. Now she could only see his thick dark hair and sense how rapidly he was breathing. Then came a moist, warm sensation which could only be his mouth moving across her, travelling across her breast in an almost intolerable intimacy. She made an involuntary sound when his tongue touched her nipple.

He looked up at her with eyes black as night. "Yes, that is what I want from you, Elizabeth." He pushed her shoulders back against the pillow then removed his nightshirt.

She had only seen his chest when it had been marred by his wound. She reached out to touch the newly healed scar still livid with colour, not yet faded to white, recalling the agony of not knowing whether he would live or die. How fortunate she was that he was still with her and she in his bed!

As he moved closer, she felt the roughness of his skin touch hers, her breasts pressed against him with an excruciating sensitivity. Almost of their own volition, her fingers found their way into his hair and she kissed him with all the love pent up inside her. His response was all that she could wish for.

He did not seem to need any lessons in what pleased her; he seemed to know just where to touch her, how to caress and kiss her to bring on those urges she had so fought against in the past. Whenever she shivered in response, he redoubled his efforts until she was burning with desire for more.

She did not know what to do with this torrent inside her, this unfamiliar ache consuming her, fuelled by the movement of his hands on her body, across her hips, finally finding their way between her legs. She tensed then, for this had always been the most difficult part for her to control in the past, but even so, she was unprepared for the intense pulse of heat his fingers created in her most private parts. Unable to stop herself, she pressed against his hand and made a strangled sound.

The movement of his fingers did not stop, but he said against her mouth, "If this is not pleasing to you, tell me."

She forced her mind to work again, no mean feat when her body was trembling with the cadenced sensation he was provoking in her. "No, sir, I am merely more embarrassed than I have ever been before."

She felt rather than saw his smile as he said, "Then let us see how much further I can embarrass you." He lowered his mouth to her breast.

How could he do this, taking control of her own body away from her? She had not thought, when he spoke of pleasure for her, that he meant such wantonness nor that she had the capacity to feel such a need.

He must have felt the increased stiffness in her, for he stopped and brushed her face with kisses. "Too embarrassed?"

"I fear so." She closed her eyes tightly, not wishing to see disapproval on his face.

Instead, she heard the warmth of his voice. "Elizabeth, stop thinking. Just feel."

Perhaps he did not realise how out of control she felt. "You wish me to be a complete wanton?"

"*Yes.*" There was a world of earnestness in his tone. "Trust me. Let me show you how this is meant to be."

Could she so let go of everything she had been taught? But his very nearness convinced her. Even if she was unsure, she would try because he wished it. As his fingers began to move again, bringing those impossible bursts of pleasure again, she abandoned herself to sensation.

Something seemed to take possession of her then, something that made her moan and writhe in response to his touch. It was like a delirium but of such intensity she could only lose herself within it. It built and built within her until her senses were in such riot she hardly knew herself, and then, with an abruptness that startled her, her body was overtaken by a consuming fire which erupted from his fingers and spread through her every extremity, leaving her shaking and crying out.

Then it was gone, leaving a pleasant lethargy in its wake and muscles which would not quite obey her. She could not comprehend it.

Darcy seemed unsurprised by what had occurred, a good sign, she supposed, that he did not disapprove. But he was still watching her intently. "Embarrassed?"

"Utterly mortified." She could laugh at herself a little now, at her own lack of understanding of herself.

"Well, *I* am delighted." There was such rich meaning in his voice that she could not doubt him. "Pleased beyond measure, and I shall show you just how pleased that is."

She opened her arms and her body to him then, feeling a certain relief at returning to ground familiar to her. But then he was within her, filling her, and bringing a fulfilment so unlike what she had experienced in the past when he possessed her that she could barely breathe. It was as if she was becoming a part of him, and he of her. She longed for more, tilting her hips to receive him better, and was rewarded when he moaned with pleasure. His hand reached down to grasp her leg, pulling it around his. As she obeyed his urging, embracing his legs with hers, he thrust into her once more, this time reaching depths she had not known she possessed. A cry burst from her lips as a sharp shock of pleasure stabbed through her, and she heard him murmur her name beside her ear, repeating it again and again as if it were a prayer.

The warmth of his body overwhelmed her, the ecstatic feeling of his skin against her own, the salty taste of his skin when she pressed her lips to his shoulder, seeking some way to express the impossible intimacy she felt. She could feel his urgency growing, that point where his needs overtook his careful self-control, but this time she felt her own control slipping as well, the coiled heat building in her once again. Apparently, he could sense it as well because his voice tightened as he said, "Yes. Yes, Elizabeth, yes."

Surely what happened earlier could not occur a second time, but she could tell this time it was coming, that uncontrollable surge of pleasure that made her arch back and cry out convulsively. As she clung helplessly to him, her body throbbing, he continued, ever faster and harder, bringing with him each time an echo of that pleasure within her until she felt faint. She whispered his name as he stiffened and a deep groan escaped his lips. Then it was over, and his body lay draped over hers.

Tears forming in her eyes, Elizabeth stroked his upturned cheek lightly with her fingertips then let her hand return to holding him close, feeling his chest expand and contract as his breathing slowed once more. For this moment, at least, he was hers alone.

Chapter 17

USUALLY, ELIZABETH WOKE TO early morning light, but the sun was well into the sky when she opened her eyes to find her husband's warm body beside hers and his arm thrown over her unclothed flesh. Instant recollection brought heat to her cheeks. She remembered her attempt the previous night to return to her room when he fell asleep, only to have him pull her closely against him and say in a drowsy voice, "Do not go." Even half-asleep, he made it more an instruction than a request, but she was beginning to understand that it would always be so, that his questions were more likely to be framed as commands. The master of Pemberley indeed.

Still, it was one thing to allow Darcy to see her unclothed form by candlelight and quite another to face the same prospect in full daylight. The thought sent her scrambling out of bed to slip into her nightdress. She found his nightshirt crumpled next to it on the floor then turned to discover her husband's eyes on her.

Darcy raised himself on his elbow. "What are you doing, Elizabeth?"

"I am hiding the evidence before poor Ferguson arrives." She smiled at him as she folded his nightshirt.

"Poor Ferguson indeed. Come back to bed, wife. I wish to embarrass you again."

"Again?" The word slipped from her lips before she realised what she was saying.

She could see him withdrawing behind his eyes. "Only if you wish it, of course," he said formally.

She did not wish to lose the ground they had gained, so she sat on the bed and boldly touched his cheek with her fingertips. "That is not what I meant. You merely took me by surprise."

His fingers were already busy untying the nightdress she had just fastened. "Do I shock you?"

She felt a flush travel down her body as he removed her shift. "Perhaps, but it does not follow that the shock must be unwelcome."

He spread kisses across her shoulder, sending tingling sensations deep within her. "Do you know, Elizabeth, I think I could learn to enjoy shocking you."

Laughter bubbled to her lips. "But it is so simple. There is hardly any sport in it, you must admit."

"Oh, no, there is great sport indeed." He moved his hand to show her exactly what he meant.

<hr />

Afterwards, he rested his hand on her waist, looking at it intently.

Uncomfortable with his eyes on her, Elizabeth said, "If you are hoping to find something, there is as yet nothing to discover."

"Yet you think…"

That stray lock of hair was dangling over his forehead again. She brushed it back gently with her fingertips; then, recalling the times she had wanted to make this small gesture but had feared his rejection, she impulsively kissed him. He looked at her with surprise.

"It is too early to know for certain, but I have reason to think it may be the case."

He began to trace small circles over her stomach. "But you are… well?"

"I am well." She wished she understood him better. His sudden terseness seemed to cover something, but whether it was pleasure or not she could not tell. Still, she did not want him to be disappointed if it proved a false alarm. "I will not know until it quickens, if it does. Until then, I can but guess."

The corners of his mouth turned down. "When will that be?"

She was tempted to laugh but sensed this was not the moment to tease. "I cannot predict it, I fear."

"I do not like to wait." He sounded almost petulant.

Since there was no other answer she could give apart from the one which clearly displeased him, Elizabeth decided to distract him from the issue. Gathering her courage, she ran her hand provocatively down his chest and scattered light kisses across his chest and neck, as he had done to her so effectively earlier. When her lips reached his ear, she whispered, "Some things may prove worth the wait."

Darcy tugged her closer to him, his arm encircling her, but before he could kiss her, a knock came at the door. It was followed by the sound of Ferguson clearing his throat. "Mr. Darcy, Lucy tells me that Mrs. Darcy's breakfast is ready for her in your sitting room."

Elizabeth hid a smile. Clearly even her shocking presence in the master's room could not stop Lucy on her appointed mission. "Thank you, Ferguson," she said, hoping she sounded as confident as the mistress of Pemberley ought.

She would have arisen then, but Darcy seemed disinclined to remove the arm that was holding her to him, so she rested her head on the comfortable solidity of his shoulder, feeling the slow rise and fall of his chest. If he found nothing embarrassing about their situation, she would try to take her cues from him.

"Do you prefer to breakfast in your room as a rule?" he asked.

"No, but I have done so the past few weeks, since Lucy feels it her duty to ensure that I eat well each morning."

"The decision should be yours, not Lucy's." He seemed to miss the point of her teasing.

She kissed the corner of his jaw, enjoying the roughness of the slight stubble on it. "I know, but in truth, she is right. My strength is better if I eat something before facing the perils of my toilette."

He released his hold on her. "Then I must not keep you from it."

She wondered if she should invite him to join her or if he would view that as an imposition. Perhaps a compromise position would be safest. "No doubt there is enough tea for two, if you would like a cup as well."

"Perhaps so." But he did not move from his position on the bed as she sat up and found her shift once more.

She quickly replaited her hair, aware that his eyes were following her. If only she could read his mood better! She could not tell whether he felt any of the closeness she did, but she could hope for it. She stood, casting him a smile over her shoulder. "I will ask Lucy to bring another cup then."

He turned back the bedcovers. Elizabeth automatically averted her eyes until he had shrugged into his green silk robe. He seemed to feel none of the discomfort she did. It would take time to accustom herself to her husband's ideas of intimacy.

Darcy followed Elizabeth into the sitting room, where Lucy had laid out Elizabeth's breakfast on the small table in front of the fire. Elizabeth was pleased to notice there were two cups.

Lucy looked questioningly at Elizabeth as she seated herself and began to pour out the tea. "No need to worry, Lucy; I have already informed Mr. Darcy about my possible condition."

Lucy's shoulders straightened. "Very well, madam."

Elizabeth handed Darcy a cup of tea. "Lucy has been a veritable tyrant in your absence, constantly insisting that I eat and rest. I suspect her of keeping a whip in the dressing room in case I misbehave."

Lucy's mouth dropped open in shock. Darcy laughed. "Well done, Lucy. I am glad to know my wife has been in capable hands."

Barely managing to regain her aplomb, Lucy dropped a quick curtsey. "Thank you, sir," she whispered, looking as if she wished to flee the room.

Elizabeth took a sip of her tea. "Lucy even threatened to report me to Mrs. Reynolds if I did not eat."

"Now that is a fearsome threat if you have ever seen Mrs. Reynolds in anger. It was a matter of great relief to me when I grew too tall for her to turn me over her knee."

Elizabeth laughed at the idea of such a sight. "Surely you were never disobedient, Mr. Darcy," she said archly.

He smiled slowly at her, a private smile, it seemed. "On the contrary, I am sure Lucy could tell you stories she has heard."

"Stop tormenting poor Lucy." Elizabeth placed a slice of bread on her plate. "Lucy, I will ring for you later, once I have convinced Mr. Darcy to torment Ferguson in your place."

"And richly he deserves it," muttered Darcy.

"What has Ferguson done?" Elizabeth was amused by his petulant look appearing once again. Lucy stole the opportunity to disappear through the door.

"Nothing of importance, though he is no doubt training Lucy in the fine art of subtle insubordination."

"There was nothing subtle about Lucy's insubordination. She stood over me and glared until I ate."

He frowned. "Why did you need to be convinced to eat?"

Elizabeth busied her hands spreading the jam on her bread. She could not tell him it was because she was afraid she had lost him, not yet at least. Fortunately, there was an easy excuse to hand. "I believe it is not uncommon for ladies in a delicate condition to find food unappetizing for a time. Fortunately, it seems to be improving now. Lucy barely needs to insist any longer."

"Are you certain? Perhaps I should send for a doctor. I do not wish to take risks with your health."

His look of concern, with that lock of hair drifting again over his forehead, was endearing. His worry, no doubt, was more for his potential heir than for her, but still it warmed her more than tea ever could. She said, "I do not believe there is any need for a doctor, and I am reluctant to draw attention to the possibility before I am certain of the outcome."

A shadow crossed his face, but he touched her shoulder gently as he said, "I hope you will inform me if it worsens again.

If there is anything that might provide you with relief, you have only to ask." He kissed her cheek lightly before departing through the adjoining door, leaving Elizabeth alone once more.

By early afternoon, the skies had clouded over and a brief shower had left raindrops sliding down the windowpanes. Inside the house, it was dark enough that Elizabeth found it difficult to read until she lit a lamp, and even then her mind would not remain on her book but instead kept returning to the previous night. She wondered whether it was on her husband's mind as well. He had not made an appearance since leaving her earlier that morning, and she found herself longing for his company. But did he long for hers, or view it as an inconvenience in the light of day?

A maid stepped into the sitting room and dropped a curtsey. "Mr. Bingley is here, madam."

"Mr. Bingley?" Elizabeth exclaimed. Setting aside her book, she rose to her feet and straightened her skirt. What was Mr. Bingley doing at Pemberley? Darcy had said nothing of a visit, but she remembered the false conclusion she had reached when Georgiana first arrived at Pemberley. This time she would make no assumptions.

Bingley had changed little since she had seen him last, nearly a year earlier. So much had happened since the night of the Netherfield ball! She had been just a girl then, a stranger to love and tragedy, and happy to believe the lies spoken by a man with handsome manners. It was oddly unsettling to see someone from that former life.

"Welcome to Pemberley, Mr. Bingley," she said.

He bowed. "Thank you, Miss Eliz... pardon me, Mrs. Darcy."

She smiled at his error. "Please, be seated. Have you travelled far?"

"From Leicester today, but I left Netherfield two days ago."

"Netherfield?" Elizabeth asked faintly. Had he returned to Meryton, then? Her thoughts immediately flew to Jane; Mr. Bingley must have seen something of her family if he was at Netherfield. Her mother would make certain of that. Suddenly, she missed the gentle green slopes of Hertfordshire. Because of Lydia's shame, she would never again see the familiar rooms of Longbourn, share secrets with Jane, or walk the shaded lanes she had loved. But there was nothing to be done for it. Her fingernails dug into her palm, but she would not let her pain show. She was Darcy's wife and the mistress of Pemberley, and she would not disgrace either of those titles. "I hope your journey was an easy one."

Darcy's tall form filled the doorframe. "Bingley! This is an unexpected pleasure." He took a seat next to Elizabeth and favoured her with a warm smile.

Bingley's mouth tightened. "I am en route to Scarborough, and there is a matter I wished to discuss with you."

"Of course. You will stay the night at least, I hope?" Darcy's smile had faded.

Elizabeth looked from Bingley's uncharacteristically serious mien to her husband's furrowed brow. Had they quarrelled? Darcy had not mentioned anything of the sort, but perhaps he was reluctant to remind her of Bingley.

"Perhaps," Bingley said.

It must be a serious quarrel then. Elizabeth rose to her feet. "If you will excuse me, gentlemen. I hope I will see you at dinner, Mr. Bingley." She left the room, closing the door behind her.

Darcy watched as Bingley paced across the sitting room. He had never seen his friend in this sort of agitation. "What is the matter?"

Bingley swung to face him. "I forgave you when you told me you had hidden Miss Bennet's presence in London from me. I forgave you for failing to tell me of your engagement until you were safely married, even if I did not understand how you could bind yourself to a family you said was beneath me. But now I see it all—you never intended to have anything to do with the Bennets, did you? I would never have thought it of you. Do you intend to cast me off too if I marry Jane?"

"What in God's name are you talking about, Bingley?"

"I am talking about my Jane, *with tears in her eyes,* asking me if I had any news of Elizabeth. How could you refuse to allow her contact with her family?"

Darcy winced, all too aware that initially he would have been glad of such an outcome. Elizabeth had been right to despise him. "I do not know what Miss Bennet told you, but Elizabeth is perfectly free to communicate with her family. Why, I dined with her aunt and uncle in London not a week ago."

"But she wrote her family and told them not to contact her! I cannot believe that Elizabeth, who walked three miles in the mud to be with Jane, is the one to desire this separation."

"She did nothing of the sort!" Even as he spoke the words, his heart sank. Another one of her ridiculous attempts to please him. "At least, not to my knowledge, and certainly not on my direction."

"But…" Bingley's shoulders slumped. "Jane would not lie to me. Perhaps she misunderstood."

There he was, the old biddable Bingley, once again believing him without question. He did not deserve such a trust. "Perhaps Elizabeth can explain it. I cannot speak for her."

Bingley shot him a odd look, as if questioning that his wife might act without his knowledge. But then, Bingley did not know the true circumstances of his marriage or how very little Elizabeth confided in him. He owed Bingley more honesty than he had given him. He rang a bell to summon a servant. "Let me send for her so we can resolve this."

It was several uncomfortable minutes before Elizabeth appeared. She appeared in good spirits. Darcy hoped she would remain so after this discussion. After their night together, the last thing he wanted was to risk losing her good opinion.

He cleared his throat. "Elizabeth, Mr. Bingley has a concern I hoped you could clarify. He thinks I have instructed you not to contact your family."

She bit her lip and glanced at Bingley. "That is not the case. I made the decision myself after… recent events."

So it was true. "Without discussing it with me?"

Her cheeks grew pale and she looked down, her hands clasping and unclasping in front of her. Then, without a word, she turned and fled the room.

It took him almost an hour to find her, and then he did so only with the assistance of Lucy, who informed him that her mistress often sat in the old grotto in the gardens. She was not on the stone bench there, as he would have expected, but just before giving up, he spotted a corner of sky blue fabric by the big elm tree. He circled the trunk to discover Elizabeth seated on the damp ground, her head tipped back against the uneven bark, her eyes closed. Her face was tear streaked.

Once again he had made her cry, just when he had begun to

think there might be hope for them. She did not love him; he knew that much. He supposed she must have developed some sort of affection for him. After all, she was naturally affectionate, as he had seen when she came to Netherfield to care for her sister, and there was no one apart from him and Georgiana for her to attach herself to now. But despite the night they had shared, she had shown no inclination for his company during the day. It ought to be enough for him to have Elizabeth in her former spirits and in his bed. Why did he always have to want more than he could have?

He knelt beside her and took her cool hand in both of his. "Elizabeth, I did not intend to upset you." He did not understand her precipitate departure or what he had said to offend her. But after the solace of a night in her arms, he could not bear to see her troubled, especially when he was at fault. She would never have taken such a step with her family had it not been for the disapproval he had expressed earlier in their marriage.

She opened her eyes and looked at him searchingly. "Did you expect me to lie on your behalf?"

Now he was completely baffled. "To lie? Of course not. I wanted to know the truth."

"The truth is that I did tell you about it, as you know well." A single tear made its way down her cheek. "It is true, I suppose, you did not agree to it, but you made no protest, either. Do not tell me you do not recall; you had not taken laudanum in days."

He shook his head helplessly. "As God is my witness, I do not recall. I would not have agreed to it. I know what your family means to you."

Her chin dropped, and he could see in her face that he had

disappointed her yet again. Desperately he said, "When did this happen? Perhaps I did not understand."

"It was the day I told you about Lydia's elopement. I gave you the letters from Jane and Lydia, and I told you I had written to my family and asked them not to contact me." Her voice was flat.

"When I was reading the letters?"

"Yes."

He could not bear to see her tears, so he gathered her into his arms. After all, she had said that it comforted her when he held her. It did not matter that whatever affection she bore him was halfhearted; it was enough, at least for now. If only he did nothing to alienate her once more. If she forgave him this. "Then the fault is wholly mine. Many people, no doubt most, can attend to a conversation while reading or doing something else; I am not one of them. I thought you knew. You can ask Bingley; he will tell you many amusing stories of how oblivious I can be. But it is not always amusing, as you have discovered."

Her head rested against his shoulder as if she were exhausted, but he felt an enormous relief when her arms stole around him. He pressed a kiss against her forehead. "Please, Elizabeth, will you write to your family tonight? I do not want this misunderstanding to persist."

She shook her head. "It is for the best this way. Even without the scandal, there is your sister to consider."

"Georgiana?"

"She told me of her history with Wickham. I cannot expose her to the comments my mother and sisters might make."

"She told you?" They must have indeed drawn closer while he was away for Georgiana to trust her with that information.

"While your concern for her is laudable, the cost to you is too high. In any case, it is immaterial. Since this business with your sister required your aunt and uncle to cancel their tour, I invited them to join us here for Christmas."

Elizabeth looked up at him, her fine eyes betraying her surprise. "You did?"

"Yes, when I dined with them in London. So it is settled. I spoke to Bingley in London, too, about your sister. I assume that is why he went to Netherfield."

She said nothing, but her arms tightened around him. It was enough.

⁂

Georgiana gazed out of the window of the sitting room. The grey clouds looming over the hills matched her mood. Why had her brother left her alone with their guest? He knew how uncomfortable she felt acting as a hostess, even with someone she knew as well as Mr. Bingley. It was not like him to abandon her, especially with only a maid as chaperone. She hoped it was not because of any intentions he might have for her future. A shiver travelled down her back. She did not want to think of marrying anyone, even a pleasant gentleman like Mr. Bingley. After watching the discomfort between her brother and Elizabeth, she was not certain she ever wanted to marry. If the frowns and silences she had seen when she first arrived at Pemberley were what she could expect of a newly wed state, it held no appeal for her. At least they had seemed more friendly since his trip to London.

She rallied herself to ask a question. "Will you be visiting family in Scarborough, Mr. Bingley?

"My aunt and uncle. My cousin is to be married next week.

My sisters are already there, but I had unfinished business I needed to conclude."

"Do you intend to stay long in the North?"

"Not long; I hope to be back in London inside the month." Mr. Bingley was staring off into the air, smiling as if he were thinking of something pleasant.

At least Mr. Bingley seemed no more inclined to courtship than she was, if that indeed was her brother's intention. She turned her eyes back to the window, where she spotted two figures walking towards the house. Fitzwilliam and Elizabeth. As she watched, her brother stopped to look down at his wife, his countenance serious, then touched her cheek. Elizabeth turned to him and said something with a smile. Fitzwilliam's face seemed to relax, then he bent to kiss her. Scandalised, Georgiana tore her eyes away. Marriage had made her brother so unpredictable!

She searched her mind for something to make conversation. "Does Miss Bingley still favour the music of Mozart?" Inwardly, she scolded herself for asking such a pointless, foolish question.

"I could not say. I am embarrassed to say I do not know the music she plays, only whether I like it or not," Bingley said ruefully.

Oh, how could Fitzwilliam do this to her? If she had to marry, could it not at least be to someone who could recognise the works of Mozart? She felt completely tongue-tied. Fortunately, Fitzwilliam and Elizabeth appeared in the doorway before the silence grew painfully long. Georgiana let out a sigh of relief.

Her brother advanced into the room. "I have solved your mystery, Bingley. Elizabeth did indeed speak to me about the matter, but I was reading an important letter at the time."

Bingley looked surprised then shook his head and laughed. "And you were completely oblivious, as usual! I should have known."

Fitzwilliam looked down at Elizabeth, as if seeking confirmation. She did not seem to want to look away once their eyes met, but finally Elizabeth said, "I had not realised my husband's attention was quite so difficult to obtain." Her warm smile mitigated any implied criticism.

"I cannot believe you have only discovered this after all these months of marriage," Bingley declared.

Elizabeth's smile slipped a bit, but Darcy spoke up before she had the chance to frame a reply. "She has had little occasion to, as Elizabeth possesses a natural talent for not interrupting, unlike many women of our acquaintance."

"But now I have a good understanding of it." Her eyes locked with her husband's again. "I intend to put the knowledge to good use by waiting until he is deep in a book to confess any sins I have committed. Then I will have the pleasure of a clean conscience, and he will be none the wiser."

Bingley said, "An excellent plan. Upon my honour, when Darcy is reading, Bonaparte and all his army could come charging through with sabres drawn, and he would take no notice!"

Elizabeth laughed. "I hope we shall never have occasion to put *that* particular theory to the test."

"Why, once at our club, I bet young William Dumbarton that he could not gain Darcy's attention when…"

"Bingley!" Darcy interrupted.

Bingley looked embarrassed. "Oh, very well. My apologies, Miss El… Mrs. Darcy. Forgive me; I still find it difficult to think of you as Mrs. Darcy."

"That is very understandable, Mr. Bingley. It took me a time to become accustomed to it myself, but now I am quite comfortable with it." Then Elizabeth and Fitzwilliam were staring at each other once again as if no one else were present. Georgiana could not imagine why; in her experience, it was more common for them to avoid each other's gaze.

Bingley smiled broadly. "I do not intend to go to any great effort to accustom myself to it, since I hope someday to claim a brother's privilege."

"Nothing could make me happier," Elizabeth said warmly.

"Nor me," Fitzwilliam added with great firmness.

Georgiana sat up straight, her heart sinking. So they did want her to marry Mr. Bingley. It was all planned, and she would have no say in the matter. She would have to leave Pemberley and live far away, wherever it was Mr. Bingley lived. Even Elizabeth, who would have been her hope for understanding, seemed to wish it. Georgiana clenched her hands together, willing herself to maintain her composure.

Mr. Bingley looked ridiculously pleased, and at that moment, Georgiana hated him. Did none of them believe she ought to be consulted? If only she dared speak her mind, but she had never been able to defy her brother's wishes, and she doubted she could begin now. But she could not bear to hear another word.

She rose to her feet, her palms damp. "Pardon me, but there is something I must attend to." Foolish, foolish, foolish. Could she not at least have thought of a suitable excuse? She hurried out of the room to the consolation of her pianoforte.

It was only a matter of minutes before Elizabeth found her. Georgiana stopped playing but did not dare lift her eyes from the keyboard.

Elizabeth stood beside the pianoforte, one hand resting on the top of it. "Is something troubling you, Georgiana?"

Georgiana closed her eyes. Somehow she had to force the words out or there was no hope. "I do not wish to marry Mr. Bingley." Her voice squeaked on the word "marry."

There was a long pause before Elizabeth spoke. "I am glad to hear that, since I believe he is planning to make my eldest sister an offer of marriage."

Georgiana's eyes flew open. "*Your* sister?"

Elizabeth smiled, then sat beside her on the bench. "Yes, *my* sister. He has admired her for some time."

Her sister! Elizabeth must think her a fool for assuming their references were to her. Mortified, Georgiana mumbled, "It is just that once, long ago, my brother mentioned something… But it is no matter."

"I expect he had different ideas once, but no longer," Elizabeth said briskly. "You need not worry."

Georgiana struggled to slow her rapid breathing. "I will try, but I know it is only a matter of time until Fitzwilliam finds someone else suitable for me."

Elizabeth took her hand between both of her own. "That is no doubt true, but I do not believe he would force you into a marriage. He would want better than that for you."

A slight hitch in Elizabeth's voice made Georgiana look at her with sudden suspicion. The first time she had met Elizabeth, she had thought her a fortune hunter because she looked so unhappy about her engagement. But now she knew that her brother's fortune meant little to Elizabeth, and she had never considered why else Elizabeth would have consented to marry Fitzwilliam. Now it was clear. Her father must have made her marry him. No wonder she had seemed so wretched, marrying a man she no doubt barely knew. She felt a wave of sympathy for what her sister-in-law must have experienced at the beginning of her engagement, before she discovered what an exemplary man Fitzwilliam was.

Perhaps there was hope after all. If Elizabeth had sympathy with her position, she might well convince Fitzwilliam to let her make her own choice if ever she wanted to marry. She had seen how carefully her brother listened to his wife's opinions.

The idea that Elizabeth might try to help her was surprisingly appealing. Georgiana did not remember her mother well, but she could recall how she trusted that her mother would always be there to protect her. She straightened her shoulders and said, "I hope Mr. Bingley and your sister will be very happy."

Elizabeth tightened her grip on Georgiana's hand then released it. "Thank you. I believe they will."

Georgiana stayed in the music room for nearly half an hour after Elizabeth departed. She practised Bach, hoping the structured phrases of the fugues would soothe her nerves. Finally, she felt composed enough to return to the sitting room. Her brother and Mr. Bingley were there partaking of some refreshments, but Elizabeth was nowhere to be seen.

It was easier to enjoy Mr. Bingley's company now that she was no longer worried about her future, but for the most part, the discussion centered on his days in Cambridge, about which she could say little. In any case, she was more comfortable listening than speaking.

It was almost an hour before Elizabeth reappeared bearing a letter with a closely written envelope. She presented it to Fitzwilliam with a flourish. "There. You may post it yourself."

He glanced down at the direction then nodded in Bingley's direction. "Thank you."

"You need not thank me for what I am happy to do!" Elizabeth said.

Georgiana wondered what this business was about and why Bingley seemed to understand it when she did not. But at least they all seemed happy, which was a pleasant change.

Mr. Bingley said, "I must say that marriage seems to agree with you, Darcy. Last winter I was beginning to wonder if we should ever see anything beyond a grim visage from you. Mrs. Darcy, I commend you on the change you have wrought in him!"

"Thank you." Elizabeth spoke quietly as she sat and took up her embroidery. "Although I doubt the credit should go to me."

Darcy smiled slightly. "It is difficult to persuade my wife to accept a compliment, no doubt because she is easily *embarrassed*."

Could he be speaking of the same Elizabeth she knew? Georgiana had seen Elizabeth in many moods but could not recall seeing her embarrassed.

Elizabeth's reaction was even more curious as she turned to stare at her husband, her cheeks nearly scarlet. It seemed to take her a moment to find her voice then she said archly, "I was of the opinion that some *gentlemen* appreciate a lady's blushes."

He appeared amused. "I can think of little I appreciate more."

Georgiana hoped this new tendency of Fitzwilliam's to speak in riddles would not last long.

Elizabeth studied her reflection in the mirror as Lucy put the finishing touches on her hair for dinner. What did Darcy think when he looked at her? Apparently, she was still able to tempt him, but how much did he find to admire beyond her appearance? He had gone to some effort to seek her out earlier to discuss her family, and he had clearly enjoyed teasing her earlier. And he had embraced her under the tree when there had been no need for it. He was not indifferent to her, and apparently, he was willing to make an attempt to improve their marriage. That was enough for now. She had all the time in the world to prove her worth to him, now that he was comfortable with his prerogatives as her husband again. She practised a welcoming smile.

Their earlier misunderstanding had shaken her confidence. When Darcy first suggested that she had not told him of her plans, she had taken it as an attempt to save face in front of his friend by denying the truth. It was a severe blow; the man she believed him to be would not lie. The disappointment she had felt when she thought her faith in him misplaced had been excruciating. Thank heavens he had an explanation, and one which made sense when she reviewed the behaviour she had observed over the year she had known him. Was it only a year? She could no longer imagine her life without him.

A knock startled her from her reverie. Elizabeth watched in the mirror as Lucy opened the door a crack to see who was there then held it open to reveal her husband. Her heart raced at the sight of him.

Lucy curtsied and disappeared. Elizabeth turned in her chair with a smile, noting that his eyes were travelling down her body. At least this time she knew what he was thinking.

He wandered over to stand beside her at her dressing table. He picked up a small bottle of cut glass and seemed to examine it in the light from the window. "I suspect Bingley will ask me tonight what you told your family in your letter."

She smiled at the question he was so studiously avoiding. "I told them I had misunderstood the situation but that you had informed me you saw no impediment to further contact."

He gently placed the bottle back on the table. "I hope they will be happy to receive it."

"I am sure they will be, just as I am happy to send it."

"I am glad to hear it." He laid his fingers against her neck just where it met her shoulders and trailed them lightly along her skin. "I want you to be happy."

Her breath caught in her throat at his touch. "And embarrassed?"

He gave a quick, devastating smile as his fingertips caressed the sensitive skin along the neckline of her dress. "Preferably. Though I ought not to have said that earlier."

"It did not trouble me, beyond a moment of shock. But as we know, you enjoy shocking me." Elizabeth struggled to keep her voice steady, though she felt as if she were melting in response to his exploring hand.

His fingers found their way under her chin, tipping it up so she looked straight at him. "True, but not usually among company." He leaned down until finally their lips touched. The taste of his kiss was sweet, but nothing could warm her more than the knowledge that he wanted to be close to her. All too soon he straightened, leaving her yearning for more. "Damned dinner," he said. "I suppose we must join the others."

Elizabeth stood and linked her hand through his arm. "I suppose we must." She looked up at him through her lashes. "Shall I expect you later then?"

His eyes darkened. "Will you come to me instead? I will not turn you away this time."

She felt a flush of heat move through her. "If you wish."

"And Elizabeth…"

She cocked her head and looked up at him archly. "Yes?"

"Do not plan to linger too long with our guest." His intent gaze could have kindled flames. "I have other plans for you."

Chapter 18

DARCY AND ELIZABETH BADE farewell to Mr. Bingley the following morning, having extracted from him a promise to stop at Pemberley on his return journey from Scarborough. Afterwards, Darcy announced his intention to attend to some correspondence. Elizabeth had prepared herself for the likelihood that once again he would not express an interest in her company and so was able to manage a pleasant smile as if it did not trouble her to be separated from him after sleeping in his arms.

The night had been a repeat of the one before, but she had been more able to enjoy sharing herself with the man she loved, even if no words of love were spoken. It was a shock to be reminded that he had no interest in resuming the part of the loving bridegroom that he had played in the early days of their marriage. It was enough to make her sadness of the past month begin to reassert itself, and she found it difficult to maintain a cheerful appearance with Georgiana. She was relieved when she could finally plead the necessity of making her tenant visits.

She felt easier when alone, or rather accompanied only by Fry, the footman, since there was no need to converse with him. Her riding no longer occupied all her attention, and instead, she could remember how her husband had looked at her the previous evening as if she were the only important thing in his world. Even though it only happened when they were in their private rooms, she still valued it and hoped it gave promise for the future.

When she arrived at the Smithson cottage, she found several women with worried faces gathered there. Concerned, she asked Mrs. Smithson if anything was the matter.

The older woman said, "It's Mary Tanner, madam. We just got word. Her baby is coming early, and her husband says he won't have the midwife in his house."

Elizabeth frowned. "He says that, does he?" Weeks of help-less anger over Mr. Tanner's treatment of his family made her temper flare. "I will go myself." She hated to think of any woman being alone at such a time.

"Bless you, Mrs. Darcy," one of the women said.

"Is Mr. Tanner there?" Elizabeth asked. She had a few things to say to him if he was.

"He's at the tavern, like always, madam. But he said he'd kill anyone who went in there." Mrs. Smithson exchanged glances with the other women.

Elizabeth lost no time in reaching the Tanner cottage. She dismissed Fry outside with a request for some assistance from Pemberley. She had no idea how long this might last—hours perhaps, or at least until Darcy discovered where she. was. Calling on tenants was one thing, but the mistress of Pemberley assisting a woman in labour might not meet with his approval. It would not be her first time; she had been present at her youngest cousin's birth and had once assisted the midwife in caring for a farmer's wife at Longbourn. She pushed aside a tinge of concern over Darcy's reaction. Surely he would understand she could not leave the poor woman to the care of her young children.

An agonised scream issued from the cottage. Elizabeth hurried inside and paused until her eyes adjusted to the dimness. The fireplace contained nothing but dead ashes. Mrs. Tanner lay in the bed, her young daughter Maggie kneeling by her side. Elizabeth hurried to her bedside, but the woman's eyes did not open to acknowledge her presence, even when she spoke her name. Frightened, she laid her hand on Mrs. Tanner's chest to ascertain that she still breathed.

The girl said, "She goes to sleep between her pains."

More likely losing consciousness, given the amount of blood on the bedding. Elizabeth's palms grew damp. Nothing in her experience had prepared her for a birth where the mother was in such straits. She was tempted to insist on the midwife's presence, but she could not protect the woman from Mr. Tanner's wrath later. If the midwife had thought it feasible, she would have been there already.

A new pain roused Mrs. Tanner from her stupor. Elizabeth stepped closer and said, "How can I help you?"

The woman shook her head weakly. No doubt she knew there was little Elizabeth could offer beyond her presence. It was her fourth confinement, and she could not fail to know the danger she was in. Still, Elizabeth encouraged her to make her best effort at pushing as each pain came, despite her fear. Each time her body went limp, Elizabeth could do nothing but pray that someone would arrive from Pemberley House who would know what to do. But until then, she was on her own with a frightened little girl. Finally, she was rewarded with the welcome sight of the baby's head crowning.

Elizabeth readied the tattered fabric which was to serve as swaddling and sent Maggie out to tell the women waiting with Mrs. Smithson that the birth was imminent. She would have to give the infant to one of them and hope they could find a wet nurse. It would be weeks before Mrs. Tanner could care for the child, even if she survived the remainder of this ordeal. In any case, she did not want Maggie to be there if there was trouble with the birth.

While assisting at a birth was not new to her, delivering a baby was a different matter. Mrs. Tanner no doubt had a better idea of it than Elizabeth, but she could not be relied upon for direction. She could only do her best and hope nature would handle most of it. She took up her station beside the bed, next to an old knife and the dirty piece of string Maggie had brought her.

Just then Sylvia, the girl who now worked at Pemberley, raced in, her hands filled with cloth. "Old Sarah is on her way, madam," she said breathlessly. She looked as if she had run the entire way from the house.

"Very good. Can you help me here? The babe is coming."

The birth itself went quickly once the baby's head was revealed. Elizabeth shifted the emerging child to release the shoulders as she remembered the Longbourn midwife doing, and the baby's body slid into her waiting hands. A girl, but tiny, her colour poor. She had not expected the infant to be quite so slippery and was glad for the straw mattress. Elizabeth chafed the baby's chest until she saw the movement of air in and out then tied off the cord.

"You have a daughter," she said. Mrs. Tanner mumbled something in reply. Elizabeth finished cutting the cord while Sylvia swaddled the baby then wiped her hands on the rags, trying to clean the blood from them.

Old Sarah from the kitchens arrived then, taking command with an ease that showed her no stranger to childbirth, engaging Sylvia in helping to deliver the afterbirth. Elizabeth, feeling suddenly superfluous, picked up the baby and held her to her chest, trying to warm her. The poor thing still hadn't made a cry, though Elizabeth could hear her breathing with odd little grunts. She looked down at the infant and was taken by surprise at the tenderness she felt for this new life. A tiny hand emerged from the swaddling. Elizabeth tried to tuck it back in, only to find her finger gripped by impossibly tiny ones. Blue eyes stared up at her from a mucus-streaked face.

She gently pried her finger free then took up a small scrap of cloth and dipped it in a basin of water. She found a stool by the window to sit upon as she washed the baby's face. The tiny mouth screwed up and let forth a mewing sound at the first touch of the cool water. Elizabeth rocked her back and forth in hopes of soothing her. "Hush, sweetheart," she said.

Maggie, who had crept in after Old Sarah's arrival, scrutinised her sister's face. "Mama said if it was a girl she'd be named for you, Mrs. Darcy."

Old Sarah was massaging Mrs. Tanner's stomach. "The bleeding's stopped at least. Mrs. Darcy, perhaps you should take the baby outside. Sylvia and I can finish up here."

Elizabeth came back from her fascination with the infant to remember her circumstances. If even the scullery maid realised the mistress of Pemberley had no business here, she ought to depart, but she felt oddly reluctant to leave Mrs. Tanner and especially to turn the baby over to someone else's care.

As she hesitated, the door to the cottage slammed open to reveal a stocky man, his clothing unkempt and his gait unsteady. Elizabeth rose to her feet. "Mr. Tanner, I presume. You have a daughter."

He scowled, and Elizabeth stepped backwards to allow him to approach his wife. "Another damned girl. I told you, no more girls!" Mrs. Tanner's eyes fluttered open, filled with fear.

"Your wife is quite ill," Elizabeth said tartly.

"I won't raise no more girls. Lazy sluts, all of them. Give me that thing." He reached for the baby in Elizabeth's arms.

She held the infant tightly to her chest. She had no intention of allowing that drunken oaf to harm the child, father or not. "There is no need for you to be concerned about her. I will make arrangements for her to be taken in by another family until your wife is well enough to care for her."

He grabbed Elizabeth's arm and held it in a punishing grip. "Give her to me!"

Elizabeth recoiled from the odour of alcohol and unwashed flesh. "Take your hands off me immediately! Do you know who I am?"

"This is *my* house!" The shadows from the window fell across Mr. Tanner's enraged face as he raised his free hand. Elizabeth heard Sylvia scream, then the door burst open to reveal two of the Pemberley footmen. But they were not quick enough to stop Mr. Tanner's hand from descending in a blow to the side of Elizabeth's face.

Through the burning pain and the ringing in her head, Elizabeth's only thought was to keep hold of the baby. She staggered backwards, her arms tightening around her burden. She barely registered the sight of the footmen tackling Mr. Tanner.

Sylvia hurried to her side. "Mrs. Darcy, are you hurt?"

Elizabeth's vision was beginning to clear. It would look foolish to deny the injury. "It is nothing a little time will not remedy."

"Here, you must sit down." Sylvia took her arm and guided her to a chair.

Elizabeth took a few deep breaths and looked down at the baby. The poor thing could understand nothing of what had transpired. Near the open door Fry and Edwards had none too gently subdued the still struggling Mr. Tanner.

A shadow appeared in the doorway as Darcy strode in, his countenance severe. Fry, apparently failing to notice his master's presence, raised his foot and delivered a sharp kick to Mr. Tanner's leg.

Darcy frowned at him. "We will have none of that, Fry."

"But, sir, he struck Mrs. Darcy." Fry's tone suggested he felt the kick was richly deserved.

Seeing the anger and disbelief on her husband's face, Elizabeth said hurriedly, "I am quite well." She turned her face, hoping the dimness would disguise any sign of the injury.

Darcy stepped in front of Mr. Tanner and glared at him, looking as if he could barely restrain his own hands. "You struck my wife," he said with savage intensity.

"Mr. Darcy, it were an accident, like." His speech was slurred.

The expression on the servants' faces must have told him it was no accident. Darcy turned to Fry. "I withdraw my objection. Take him away and lock him up."

Fry twisted Tanner's arm behind him until he yelped in pain then dragged him towards the doorway. "You heard Mr. Darcy. Go!"

Sylvia cast a timid glance at Mr. Darcy, then silently took the infant from Elizabeth.

Elizabeth's arms felt surprisingly empty without the baby's weight in them. She winced inwardly at the angry look in Darcy's eyes and turned to Old Sarah to ask what might be needed for Mrs. Tanner's further care.

"Aye, just tell Mrs. Reynolds and she'll know what's needed." Old Sarah gathered up the bloody rags and dropped them in a bucket of water.

Behind her, Sylvia made a sharp noise. Elizabeth turned to see her look of dismay as Sylvia carefully loosened the swaddling over the baby's scalp and laid the cloth across her face.

Darcy was forgotten completely as Elizabeth hurried to her side. Sylvia shook her head silently. Elizabeth reached for a corner of the cloth and lifted it a few inches. The eyes that had looked at her before were staring emptily now, the pale skin turned to a sickly shade of blue. Hot tears formed in the corner of Elizabeth's eyes, and she touched the baby's cheek, then ran her finger over the little hand that lay limp now. Reluctantly, she replaced the cloth over the tiny face. "I am so very sorry." She was not certain to whom she was speaking; Mrs. Tanner was not conscious enough to know what had occurred.

"Come, Elizabeth. Let us return to the house." Darcy's expression was stern.

With a reluctant glance back at Mrs. Tanner, Elizabeth followed him outside. The day seemed surprisingly bright after the shadows of the cottage. Pandora was still tethered to the tree where Elizabeth had left her a lifetime ago, and by her side stood Hurricane, wearing bit and bridle but no saddle.

Elizabeth stopped short and turned to her husband in disbelief. "You rode *that* horse bareback?"

"I wanted to reach you quickly. Saddling takes time, and I have ridden without a saddle many times."

It was too much, on top of all the fears of the past hours, of watching life given and then snatched away. Tears in her eyes, Elizabeth said fiercely, "I *hate* that horse. I *hate* it that you still ride him. I *hate* him."

"Elizabeth," he said, as if trying to calm a fractious child, "I know how to manage a horse."

She dashed away the tears with her knuckles. "He almost killed you. You nearly died." She took a gulp of air, trying to fight back sobs, conscious that she was creating a scene.

His arms came around her, and she buried her face in his shoulder, comforted by the warmth and familiar scent of him. He said, "I am perfectly well now."

"By God's grace only. I thought you were going to die." She could not completely control her tears. "I *hate* him."

She felt his hand stroking her hair, her cheek. "On that, you have made yourself quite clear, madam."

His formality reminded her they were in public. She straightened her shoulders and stepped away. "Shall we go, then?" She did not know how she would bear watching him mount Hurricane.

"Would you prefer to walk? One of the stable boys can bring the horses back."

Almost sick with relief, she nodded, unwilling to trust her voice.

"Then let us walk." He offered her his arm.

She took it and walked beside him, too embarrassed to look at him. Between her foolish display and the inappropriate situation, he had more than enough reason to be angry with her. He said nothing either, and she kept her eyes on the ground.

When they reached the house, Darcy asked her to join him in his study once she had rested and refreshed herself. She could not help feeling like a child being called in for a scolding, except this would hurt more because it came from him. After all they had shared the last two nights, she was back where she had begun.

In the shelter of her room, she washed her hands again, trying to scrub them clean of the odour of birth and death. Lucy hurried in and clucked at the state of her apparel but made no comment on the bloodstains. She must have heard the story already. With the maid's assistance, she changed into a fresh dress, a dove grey one that matched her mood, then sat obediently as Lucy tried to coax her hair into some order.

A knock at the door announced the presence of Mrs. Reynolds, who was bearing an unrequested poultice for Elizabeth's face. So the details of the incident had spread as well. Although her jaw still stung, she did not think it required a poultice. But her husband might be angry if she refused the treatment, so she submitted to Mrs. Reynolds's ministrations.

Elizabeth held the poultice to her cheek. "Mrs. Reynolds, would you be so kind as to arrange for some assistance to be sent to Mrs. Tanner? Clothes for her and the children, I think, and blankets, as well as food."

"Already done, madam. Old Sarah will stay to help Mrs. Tanner, and she knows to send word if they need anything." The housekeeper raised the poultice and examined the swelling underneath it. "Lucy, we'll be wanting some powder to cover this before Mr. Darcy sees it again. No need to distress him further."

At another time, Elizabeth might have resented being managed to this degree, but at the moment, she was relieved someone else was making the decisions for her, especially if Darcy was as angry as Mrs. Reynolds's words suggested.

Mrs. Reynolds paused, then put her hand on Elizabeth's arm. "It was a fine thing you did, Mrs. Darcy."

It helped to know someone thought so, even if her husband did not.

A few minutes later, as Elizabeth approached Darcy's study, she wished she could turn time back. She had been so happy with the progress they had made and the affection he had shown her, and now he was angry again. The despair of the last weeks returned to flood her. Would she ever manage to keep his good opinion for long, or would it always be a series of struggles? And she could not even blame him. But she might as well face the worst. Wearily, she knocked on the door.

Darcy opened it and held it for her with courtesy, but as soon as he closed it behind him, his face lost its careful neutrality. "Elizabeth, what were you thinking, to confront such a man? Did you not consider the danger?"

She drew in a careful breath. "I considered the danger to the infant to be more serious than any danger to me."

"That is admirable but unacceptable. I will not have you risking yourself." He paced back and forth. "You are the mistress of Pemberley, not a servant. And if there is a chance you are with child, you must be that much more careful."

She sat in the leather armchair so she could avoid seeing his face. Her back straight, she said, "What would you have had me do? Allow him to hurt the infant?"

"You ought not to have been there without a manservant to protect you! Then the danger would never have arisen."

"Fry was with me earlier, but I could hardly bring a

footman into a birthing room, nor did I have any reason to fear for myself. I did not anticipate Mr. Tanner's presence. He had never been there before when I visited." She struggled to keep a quaver from her voice. Once again she was little more than a problem to him. The sting of hopelessness was painful in its familiarity.

"In future, I expect you always to be accompanied or not to go. Is that clear?"

Her cheeks burned. She would almost rather he hit her than treat her with this disdain. "Completely, sir."

Something in her voice must have struck him, for he stopped his pacing suddenly and his brow knitted. He knelt before her. "I do not wish to quarrel with you. He could have hurt you seriously or even killed you had he a mind to it."

She turned her head to the side, hiding the bruise. "And would that not be the best thing for everyone? It would solve a myriad of problems."

There was a measured pause. "What do you mean by that?"

Her bitterness would not be contained. "Why, he would hang for it and cause no more trouble. You would be free to marry again to a woman who would make you happy and beget an heir without tainted connections."

His hands gripped her arms tightly. "Elizabeth, do not say such things! Not ever."

"Very well. In future I will only *think* them."

"Christ in heaven, Elizabeth! Are you trying to drive me mad?"

She was about to make an angry retort when the pain in his face struck her. "No," she said tiredly. She rose to her feet and walked to the far end of the room, facing away from him. "I will be reasonable now and go back to pretending all is well and that

I believe you are content in our marriage. I will do my best to avoid danger in future and always take a servant with me when I call on tenants. I will even pretend I do not hate your horse. Is that satisfactory?"

The silence was like a leaden weight. "I will stop riding Hurricane. It is the only thing you have ever asked of me."

It was the last thing she expected him to say. She put her hands over her eyes and burst into tears.

She heard his footsteps, and then his arms came around her. The warmth of his breath caressed her forehead as he spoke. "I am sorry, Elizabeth. I had thought you happier of late, but obviously I have been deceiving myself. There is nothing I can do to make up for the pain I have caused you. All I can do is to ask you what I might do, what I might change to make you less miserable. Ask, and I will do it, whatever it might be."

Elizabeth could not even think to respond. He was a good man, and she should not have spoken to him as she did. "I *am* happier. What happened earlier..." She faltered as an image of the baby's face presented itself in her mind, a life that would never be lived, a child who would never play outside in the sunshine. She gripped Darcy's shoulders tightly, unable to breathe.

"Elizabeth, what is the matter?"

She could not help leaning into his embrace, sobbing for everything that had been lost. "She was so very tiny. The baby..."

His hand stroked her back comfortingly until her sobs subsided. "I am sorry you had to witness that, to have it add to your unhappiness."

He did not understand, but perhaps no man could. She wiped her eyes. "It was frightening, and I have not yet fully recovered my spirits. Please do not take that to mean I am unhappy in general."

"This is why I do not want you in such a situation."

"I have said I will not do it again."

"So you have." He released her but did not walk away. "But my question remains—what can I do to make you happier?"

His intensity made her uncomfortable. "Truly, I am quite content. I need nothing beyond what I have. But I thank you for the offer. Shall I see you at dinner, then?"

His hand gripped her arm. "No, Elizabeth. We are not done yet. I have let you slip away too often when you say all is well. You are not leaving until you have asked something of me."

"But there is nothing I want or need. You have always been generous."

"I am not speaking of trinkets. What can I do that will make you happier?"

What was she to ask when the only thing she wanted was his love? But that could only be given, not asked for. "I do not know."

"There must be something you would like that I have never done."

Once, he had loved her. Still, she had to answer him. Perhaps she could ask for something that would help her understand him better. "You could tell me about your brother."

His expression of surprise was replaced quickly by dismay. "How will *that* make you happier?"

Elizabeth's first impulse was to tell him he need not do it, but she recalled it was his insistence that she ask for something. "I do not know yet, but I do not like secrets."

He ran his hand through his hair. "It is not a secret, just something we do not speak of."

"It is a secret to me."

"Very well." He crossed the room and poured himself a large brandy. She did not recall seeing him drink this early in the day before. He settled himself on the brown leather loveseat. "What is it you wish to know?"

"I know nothing about him but his name."

"Well, then. He was two years my junior and my closest friend in my youth, though we could not have been more opposite. I was serious; he was merry. I was cautious; he was bold. I disliked meeting new people; he loved it. But there was no one whose company I preferred." He fell silent, gazing intently into his glass. "There was one other difference as well. He liked George Wickham; I did not, but I pretended to for Thomas' sake."

She had no wish to discuss Wickham. "Did you spend much time with Thomas?"

"Whenever we could. We had lessons together and rode with our mother. Later, when my father insisted on my involvement in the business of the estate, Thomas ended up in scrapes, usually aided, if not led, by George. He had no malice in him, just the high spirits of youth. George had more cruelty in him, but Thomas never saw it."

"What happened then?"

He took a swallow of brandy. "Nothing in particular. I went to Cambridge, and I missed Thomas. He was due to join me in two years, and I looked forward to it. But there was an outbreak of smallpox that winter. Neither Thomas nor my mother survived. I knew nothing of it until it was all over, and when I returned…" He paused, his attention seemingly on swirling the brandy in the glass.

She had the feeling he had forgotten her presence. "What happened when you returned?"

"Nothing. Thomas was always my father's favourite, and I my mother's. My father did not find me an adequate substitute for Thomas. I suppose I resented my father as well for surviving when my mother had died and for seeking his comfort in George Wickham's company. Then two years later, my father died of apoplexy, equally unexpectedly, while I was in London. So if I seem to worry excessively over your safety, perhaps that is why."

She nodded slowly. "That is enough to make anyone worry. I am grateful to be back on the list of people you worry about."

"Back?"

Elizabeth shifted uncomfortably. "I believe there was a time after our quarrel when you would have been just as happy had I disappeared into the mist!" she said, trying to turn it into a jest.

"No, never that. I was angry perhaps at first, but my anger soon began to take a proper direction when I realised what I had unwittingly done. I never stopped loving you."

The assertion was so startling and matter-of-fact that Elizabeth could not believe it at first, much less take pleasure in it. "But you…"

"I know; what I feel hardly signifies when it has caused you so much pain. I do not even know how to begin to beg your forgiveness for what I have done to you."

"There is nothing to forgive," she said, still struggling to take in his startling assertion. "But do you not regret marrying me?"

Darcy stood and walked over to the window, looking out over the Pemberley grounds. "That is a difficult question, for the answer is both yes and no. Yes, in that I would not do it again because of the pain it caused you. I wanted to make you happy, and instead,

I made you suffer. But, as you know, I can be very selfish. Can I bring myself to regret having you as my wife? No, I cannot."

She would never forget this moment or the flood of relief it unleashed in her. She went to him and put her arms around him. "I do not regret it either, nor do I regret loving you."

She felt the breath catch in his chest. "Are you trying to assuage my guilt or do you truly mean that?"

She tipped her head back to look up at him. "Of course I mean it. Do you think I could have given myself to you as I have these past two nights if I did not love you?"

He searched her eyes, then his arms crushed her to him almost painfully. "I can speak of this no more, Elizabeth. You do not know how I have suffered for what I have done."

She put her finger to his lips. "Then do not speak of it. Shall I leave you for now?"

"No." He held her tightly, as if he feared she might disappear. "Do not go."

Chapter 19

AFTER SUPPER, DARCY ANNOUNCED that he was fatigued and would be retiring early, giving a significant glance to Elizabeth. Slightly bemused, she accompanied him when he returned to their rooms. But instead of taking her to his room as she expected, he stopped in their private sitting room, leading her to the sofa by the fireplace. He invited her to sit with him and put his arms around her, encouraging her to lean her head against his shoulder.

Elizabeth hid a smile. "This is why you wished to retire early?"

He flushed. "I found I did not want to share your company with Georgiana this evening. We had so little time this afternoon and much yet to be said."

She heard the slight doubt in his voice. "I am perfectly happy to have you to myself as well, especially since for so long I could not."

He seemed content just to sit and hold her, but after a few minutes he said, "May I ask you a question?"

"Of course."

"You often seem frightened of me, and I have wondered why. I like to think I have not mistreated you."

"No, of course you have not." She hesitated before answering, fearing her response might displease him. "But you yourself said you were of a resentful temper. The lies Wickham told me convinced me you could be ruthless when angered. I saw how you did not hesitate to show your disdain. I did not know what you would do if I disappointed you, and as your wife, I was totally in your power." She paused. "As I still am."

His lips tightened. "But you must know I would not abuse that power."

"I know that now. But I still fear displeasing you, for I never know what will make you turn me away."

"You need not worry. Nothing could do that."

Her instinct was to remain silent, but hiding her feelings had not served her well with him. "But you have often rebuffed me when I approached you."

"What do you mean?" He sounded more puzzled than irritated.

"Whenever I took the initiative to approach you—when I thanked you for the necklace, or when I greeted you on your return from London, or when I wrote you that letter—it angered you. You cannot deny it."

"But I was not angry with *you*." He sounded more than a little annoyed by her suggestion.

"It certainly seemed so to me."

His arms tightened around her. "Do you know what it is to be a man violently in love? To live for a woman's smiles and laughter, to hunger for her touch until life itself seems impossible without it, to desire her as you desire to breathe? I was angry and hurt after our quarrel, yes, but it did not take long for those other feelings to resurface, and then…" He abruptly turned his face away from her.

Elizabeth felt a moment of panic then forced herself to remember how he had told her of his love just that afternoon. She ran her finger down his cheek. "And then?"

The words began to tumble out, like water behind a breached dam. "Then I faced an impossible temptation. You would give me anything I asked for. I could have all those things I wanted so badly, merely by indicating to you I wanted them. You would smile and laugh for me and welcome me to your bed, but it would not be out of affection on your part, merely duty." He said the last word as if it were poison.

"But I told you I loved you in my letter and many times while you were ill."

"I thought it an attempt to please me. I wanted you so badly that sometimes I was almost willing to accept what I was certain were lies. So I rejected your advances before I reached the point where I would take advantage of your deference to my wishes. It was… a struggle."

"But it was not duty! Did it never occur to you that I might come to care for you?"

He sighed heavily. "No. It did not." His words held a great finality.

She ran her fingers over his brow, wishing she could wipe away the furrows. This was her doing. "You undervalue yourself. I have found much to admire in you."

"I thank you, but your admiration was not what I sought. But it is nothing new. I have not the gift of winning friendships. When I meet people, I am constantly giving offence, often without intending to do so. There are few people willing to overlook that, and those who do seek my friendship tend to be looking for an advantage in it. You were different. When I said the wrong thing, you would laugh and turn it back around at me. It did not seem to trouble you. But I was wrong about that, as I have been wrong about so many other things."

It explained how her lively spirits had misled him, something she had often wondered about, but his first words had surprised her. "But you have friends, and you are respected by everyone here at Pemberley."

"Very few true friends and most are like Bingley, who cannot hold a grudge for long even on the rare occasions he takes offence. But you know my weakness already; I certainly offended you often enough on the matter of your family when I thought it showed that I trusted you. Instead, I only made you dislike me more." Darcy stood and moved to the fireside, taking up a poker and stirring the flames. A log crackled and broke, sending a spray of sparks up the chimney.

Because he trusted her. If she wanted him to trust her again, she must tell him the truth, no matter how painful. "It angered me when you said those things because they were true. My family has been embarrassing me since I was old enough to understand what embarrassment meant. I learned in time to laugh at it, since the only other choice was perpetual mortification and fearing the world's opinions. I love my family dearly, but I resented you for speaking the truth about them."

She could not look at him. The roots of this shame went deep, back to her childhood when she began to recognise that some of their acquaintances turned away when her mother approached them. She had learned to observe those people, to watch their more seemly behaviour, and to emulate it, so no one would look at her as they did at her mother.

Now he knew her secret. She raised her eyes to his face. "Will you forgive my pride for refusing to acknowledge your qualms about my family?"

Darcy shook his head. "I am the one who should beg forgiveness. I ought never to have said those things. I should have realised it would hurt you. There is unseemly behaviour enough among my relations, but the difference is that no one dares condemn them for it. It would be different, I am sure, had they not the Fitzwilliam name to protect them."

She remembered how she had thrown the same accusation at him during their quarrel, before she knew how deeply she could injure him, before she understood the vulnerabilities that lay behind his sometimes autocratic front. Even now with their better understanding, she could still see the sadness behind his eyes and knew herself to be the cause. If only she could drive it away as easily as she had caused it.

But perhaps she could, for she knew what he liked. She gave him an arch look as she wound her arms around his neck. "I love my family, but perhaps it is as well that we do not live *too* close to Longbourn." She leaned in to caress his lips with hers.

He put his hand behind her head, ensuring that she did not escape the kiss quickly. "Nor too close to Rosings, I might add."

It was a small triumph to hear him more cheerful again, for it was still easy to shake her faith in his love for her. The pain that thought gave her drove her to seek the reassurance of closeness to him. Her hands reached for his waistcoat, unfastening the buttons so she could feel the warmth of him through the thin lawn of his shirt. She leaned her head against his chest with a sigh.

His eyebrows shot up. "You never cease to amaze me, Elizabeth."

"What, am I shocking you, sir?"

He drew in a sharp breath. "Yes. But pleasantly so."

She had not intended anything beyond what she had already achieved, but his look spurred her to try her luck at untying his immaculate cravat. "Would that be more or less pleasant than you find shocking me to be?" She nibbled on his lower lip, successfully keeping him from responding immediately.

"I am not certain as yet," he said, his voice a little ragged. "You had best continue, in order to give me sufficient evidence to consider the question."

"I certainly cannot stand in the way of scientific inquiry," she teased as she tugged at a particularly difficult knot in his cravat. Finally, it gave way and the white cloth came free in her hands.

She so rarely had the opportunity to see his neck, and she loved the lines of it. She ran her fingers from the corner of his jaw down to the base of it. Overtaken by a sudden burst of love for him, she pressed her lips to his neck, where his pulse ran below the surface, tasting the salt of his skin. She untied his shirt at the collar and slipped her hand inside to caress his chest.

His hands reached for her breasts. Without thought, she pressed herself forward into his touch. It was hard to remember that only a few days earlier she would have shied away from this sensation, and now she sought it out as his thumbs rubbed across the sensitive tips, making her ache for him. She pushed back his coats to bury her face against his shirt, breathing in his musky scent, impatient to remove that last barrier.

She had started this for his sake, but it had turned to something else. She wanted the closeness to him for herself, to feel the joy of her love for him and to forget the pain and fear of the day in the pleasure he could give her, to remember life when there had been death. She tugged at his shirt until it came free of the waistband of his trousers.

"Elizabeth." Darcy spoke her name as if it were a plea. His mouth sought out hers, tasting her as if he could never have enough. "Tell me this is real and not another dream."

Her response was half-laugh, half-sob. "It is real." She could feel his arousal beneath her, making her long to be connected to him in the most intimate of ways and never to part. "Come." She stood on trembling legs and took his hand, leading him to her room.

He paused in the doorway. "Shall we go to my room instead?"

"Do you dislike it here?" She had wondered why he had wanted her in his bed the last two nights.

"No, but I do not wish to remind you... of before." He said it quietly, as if not wanting to give the words too much power.

She turned and put her arms around him, touched by his concern for her. "It will not remind me because I understand now what it is to love you. You need have no fear of the past."

Her words seemed to mobilise him. He stripped off his topcoat and waistcoat, tossing them carelessly over a chair, then reached for the buttons at the back of her dress. Elizabeth could not stop watching his form. The draped fabric of his shirt revealed his shape more than his coat ever did.

His hands moving industriously down her back made her tremble with anticipation as he freed her first of her dress, then her corset and shift. It was as if he could not wait; as soon as she felt the coolness of the air against her skin, his hands began roaming over her exposed flesh. She gasped as the sensation threatened to consume her.

"Bed," he said succinctly.

With an arch smile she led him there, letting him press her back against the pillows. His urgency was unmistakable, and her own was hardly less. She strained against him, seeking to be ever closer, to feel the very essence of him.

He held himself still as his hand wandered between her legs, arousing her yet further as his fingers brushed against her most private places. The previous nights, he had lingered there to give her pleasure, but tonight she needed a different sort of fulfilment. She did not yet know how to communicate her desire by touching him, so instead she begged, "Please love me, Fitzwilliam."

He stilled then, and she could see the fine sheen of perspiration on his chest. He must have been trying to hold back for her sake. A surge of love for him overwhelmed her as he parted her legs with his own.

"Now and always, my love," he whispered, his breath warm against her ear. Then he was within her, moving in an instinctive rhythm she could not resist.

This was not how she had ever imagined love to be, but now she knew what it meant to give herself utterly to the man she loved, unclothed both in body and soul. At first she could only glory in the sense of intimacy she felt with him; and the release of her fears of losing his love, still with her from that afternoon, brought her near tears. Then she abandoned herself to the gift of pleasure, sensing Darcy's satisfaction as he made her moan and move beneath him. Waves of heat began to wash through her, building ever higher as she opened herself to him even more, until they finally crested in a spiral of sensation that left her trembling.

Afterwards, she savoured his closeness as he cradled her in

his arms. She brushed her lips against his. "Now do you believe it is real?" she asked.

"Yes, but I will not object if you tell me again." He twined his fingers in her curls, looking as if he were studying them intently.

The words she had thought she could never say now came freely to her lips. "I love you ardently and with all my heart."

Looking up at him, she thought his eyes were glistening.

❧

Darcy asked the boy at the stable to fetch Pandora and Mercury. In response to Elizabeth's grateful glance, he said, "I told you I would not ride Hurricane. I think you will approve of Mercury."

Elizabeth bit her lip. "Do you mind terribly?"

"Not if it pleases you, my love." He would miss Hurricane, but Elizabeth's happiness was paramount.

Hoofbeats sounded behind them. Georgiana, her cheeks rosy, trotted up on her tall mare. "I did not realise you would be riding today, Fitzwilliam. Perhaps you would enjoy a race?"

He sought out Elizabeth's hand. "Thank you, but another time. I am planning to ride with Elizabeth."

"Elizabeth could join us."

Elizabeth shook her head. "I fear not. I am still a beginner, and I doubt either of you would be interested in the pace I keep."

Georgiana's mare stamped her feet, and the girl expertly guided her a few feet away. "How is it you never learned to ride before?" It was clear she had been longing for an opportunity to ask the question.

"I did not care to. Once, when I was small, I was playing by the lane, and I saw a man thrown from his horse. He died at my feet."

Darcy turned to her in surprise. "You never told me he died." It explained something of the depth of her mystifying fear of horses. And he had pushed her to learn, without realising what he was asking. "Are you certain you wish to do this?"

She turned a luminous smile on him. "Of course. How can I resist the opportunity to visit the famous Curbar Edge?"

His heart filled with admiration of her. "It will be a long ride at a walk."

"Then it is a fortunate thing I will have good company."

Georgiana watched as they mounted their horses and ambled away. She would die of boredom on Elizabeth's horse. At least that solved one mystery about Elizabeth, but Georgiana doubted she would ever understand her brother's marriage. First they barely talked to one another, and now suddenly they were inseparable. It was quite baffling. Without question, she was in no hurry to marry.

❧

The ride proceeded without event. Elizabeth was grateful that Mercury, while solid with muscle, was obedient to Darcy's commands and did not strain at the reins as Hurricane had. Darcy had been correct about teaching her to ride though; even for a great walker, the ascent up the steep incline would be a challenge on foot.

The view from the top of the Edge was as spectacular as Darcy had promised—across fields, river, and wild pasture. She could make out the narrow, winding road through the glen and the small white dots that were grazing sheep. The wind, no longer fettered by the surrounding hills, whipped past her cheeks as she clambered onto one of the rock formations that lined the cliff edge. Exhilarated by the raw power of nature around her, she was sorry when she heard her husband's voice calling her after only a few minutes. When she looked back at him, he was holding out his hand to her from the moor at the edge of the rocks.

When she reached him, she was struck by the pallor of his cheeks. "Are you well?" she asked.

He heaved a deep sigh. "If this is anything similar to what you experienced when I rode Hurricane, I am sorry I ever went near him."

With sudden understanding, she said, "I had forgotten you disliked heights."

He pulled her into his arms. "It is worse to see you there than it is to be there myself."

"But I thought this was a favourite spot of yours."

"It is, when I am a safe distance from the edge." He did not say anything for a moment, just held her, stroking her hair. "I used to come here with my mother and Thomas. He was like you, unafraid to climb to the very rim of the rocks. He would tease me by holding his arms over the side as if he were going to step off, but my mother would make him stop."

He was telling her about Thomas, whom he had said was never mentioned. She looked up into his dear face. "How I love you!"

He raised an eyebrow. "I am not certain what I did to deserve that, but I will accept it gladly." He kissed her lingeringly.

"I am glad you are telling me about your family."

His body tightened within her arms, and she wondered if she had said too much. His eyes seemed fixed on the distance beyond the cliff. "Once, when I returned to Pemberley after their deaths, I came here alone. I did not plan to return."

She could not hide her horror. Her voice shook a little when she said, "I am very grateful you changed your mind."

He shrugged. "I wanted the loneliness to end, and I could see no way out of it. My father was caught up in his own grief, and Georgiana was but a little girl I barely knew. But in the end, I could not do it. Too many responsibilities."

Elizabeth remembered the night she had sought out the bottle of laudanum, only to be stopped by *her* responsibilities at a time when death seemed preferable to living. "That must have been a very dark time." She could not imagine the world without him, having feared losing him so much during his illness. Suddenly, she straightened, a frightening suspicion in her mind. "Fitzwilliam, is this not where you were when you injured yourself?"

For a moment he looked confused, then his eyes cleared. "No, the fall was not intentional, if that is what you are asking. I was angry, and I confess the thought crossed my mind as the simplest route to give you back your happiness, but I dismissed it quickly. Here on the Edge, I realised the difference between our quarrel and Thomas's death. I would never see him again, but with you there was still hope, no matter how far-fetched it seemed at the moment." He paused as the wind blew tendrils of her hair across his face then said in a different tone, "I will confess I was perhaps riding a bit recklessly, given the terrain."

"Now that I have no difficulty believing!" Elizabeth exclaimed. "Though I do not care to imagine what might constitute reckless riding for you, since I see it in the riding you do every day."

He laughed. "I will take more care, for your sake. But now, I should take you out of this wind before you catch a chill."

"I am not so fragile as that!" she said, but she allowed him to lead her to the horses.

He put his hands on her waist, but did not boost her to the saddle as she had expected. "Do you still fear it? Riding, that is?"

"Occasionally, but for the most part, no."

"When we return to level ground, would you be willing to try trotting? It is truly quite safe. But only if it will not trouble you." He looked like a little boy asking a favour.

"I will *try* it, but I may not *continue*."

"As I said once before, that is all I can ask." He kissed her before lifting her atop Pandora.

Darcy led the way down the steep hill, allowing Elizabeth to admire the fine figure her husband cut on horseback. She wondered how she could have ever failed to be aware of how handsome he was.

When they reached the valley, intersected by a bubbling stream, Darcy halted his horse and dismounted, then held a hand out to Elizabeth. She slid down Pandora's flank, pausing to pat the horse's head when her feet were safely on the ground.

"No trotting?" she asked.

"I thought perhaps we should rest a little first. It has been a long ride, and I do not want to overtire you, especially under the circumstances."

"If you wish, though I could continue easily enough." Elizabeth found a patch of soft grass to sit upon while Darcy tied the horses to a sapling. "I am glad to take advantage of the fair weather. Soon it will be winter, and if I am indeed with child, I will not have this freedom."

He sat beside her, then stretched out on the ground, his hands behind his head. "Do you think often about that possibility?"

She smiled at the obvious care he took in choosing his words. "To be quite honest, I have not thought about it as much as I would have expected, having been preoccupied with other matters. But I was excited to tell you about it. I thought you would be pleased."

"Not *that* again!"

"What is wrong with wishing to please you? Do you not wish to please me?"

"Yes, I suppose. But I have been concerned because you seemed so indifferent to the possibility. I feared you might resent it."

Elizabeth felt a wave of guilt at his perspicacity. She plucked a stem of grass and folded it between her fingers. "Perhaps a little at first but not now."

She could see her reply had disappointed him. "What changed your mind?"

Uncomfortably she said, "It was a shock initially."

In a fluid movement he sat up and at the same time pressed her backwards so that he leaned over her, propped up on his elbow. "For the rest of our lives, Elizabeth, it is going to worry me when I feel that you are avoiding telling me something."

She gazed into his dark eyes, seeing the concern there. She turned her head to the side with a sigh. "This is difficult to speak of."

He did not move or say anything, just entwined his fingers with hers.

He had told her the truth of his despair, and she was honoured that he had trusted her with it. She owed him her truth as well, although she feared it might hurt him. She would simply have to reassure him to the best of her ability. "Very well, if you must know, I was distraught at the time, not from the realisation I might be with child but before that. I misunderstood why you went to London, thinking you did it to avoid my company. I did not wish to live. The baby meant I had no choice but to go on living. Now I see it differently, but, then, it was hard."

A look of horrified comprehension came over his face. "I will never forgive myself."

She placed her hands on each side of his face, forcing him to meet her gaze. "Do not blame yourself. It was a failure of understanding, nothing more. When I look back on it, I can see you must have thought it clear why you were leaving."

"I was sure you knew I was going to find your sister. And I still cannot comprehend why you thought I no longer loved you. It is not something I could change."

"I had given you reason to hate me, and you were so distant."

He shook his head. "Distant? I knew how much you disliked me. I thought to spare you the burden of my company, at least as much as possible in civility."

Impulsively, she reached up to kiss him. "And I wished only for the opportunity to show you I regretted my errors."

"We have been at such cross-purposes, my love, and I have caused you so much pain. I do not know how you can forgive me."

"I have been your equal in misunderstandings. But while I would not deny that I have been unhappy, if I had not learnt what it meant to lose you, I would not have realised what you meant to me. Or at least to think I had lost you. I still cannot understand how you can forgive me for the things I said to you."

"How could I not, given all the mistakes I have made? I had known something was troubling you, that you were not yourself. I should have realised much sooner that *I* was the problem."

"Let us not argue any further for the greater share of blame, but instead, think of the pleasures of the present. But there is one thing I must thank you for."

"What is that?"

She gave him a teasing look. "For kissing me that day at Rosings. If you had not, I would have refused you and said something quite intemperate, and we would have parted in anger, never to meet again. I should have missed so much had I never discovered the man you truly are."

He put his arms around her, burying his face in her hair. "It is I who ought to thank you."

⁂

Darcy frowned. It was completely ridiculous for him to feel abandoned simply because Elizabeth had decided to visit the convalescent Mrs. Tanner and some of the other tenants. Still, he had to force himself to allow her go alone or at least only in the company of a footman and a maid. He could not hover over her every minute. Even knowing there was no danger, as Mr. Tanner was in the magistrate's hands and would never return to Pemberley, he disliked having her away from his side.

The urgent knocking at the study door caught Darcy's attention immediately. He put aside the letter he was writing and called, "Yes?"

It was the servant girl Sylvia, the one Elizabeth had taken such an interest in. She was breathing heavily, as though she had been running. Darcy's brows furrowed at her interruption. As a housemaid, she ought to know better by now.

"Mr. Darcy, sir, Mrs. Darcy is down at my family's house, and she's talking to a man, and I don't think she likes him. And she told me I was to come back right away and report to you, even though I was supposed to be helping her, so I think she wanted me to tell you."

Not tenant trouble again. Elizabeth would know better, would she not? Still, he rose to his feet as he said, "Who is this man?"

"My mother's cousin, sir. He's visiting from London with his wife, and they know Mrs. Darcy. His wife *says* she is Mrs. Darcy's sister." Sylvia's disbelief in this claim was readily apparent.

Her mother's cousin. Suddenly he remembered why the name Smithson was familiar. He strode to the door. "Show me where she is."

Fortunately it was not far. He knew better than to take a fast horse this time, and despite his instinct to tear Elizabeth away from Wickham, he knew it was not Wickham's way to harm her physically. No, Wickham was nothing but an opportunist. It was the lies he would tell Elizabeth that he needed to worry about. She had believed him before, and he knew all too well how convincing Wickham could be when he set his mind to it. Georgiana was proof of that.

Darcy stopped short. The girl looked at him questioningly. "Sylvia, I have changed my mind. Please go back to the house, and tell Mrs. Reynolds—no one else, mind you!—that Miss Darcy is not to leave the house until I have returned."

"Yes, sir." She pointed down the road. "Our cottage is the next one behind the hedgerow." She bobbed a curtsey and turned towards Pemberley House. Darcy strode forward without looking back.

Elizabeth tried to quell her rising indignation. "Mr. Wickham, I believe my husband has *already* been generous enough to purchase your commission." She could hardly credit the easy assurance with which he bore himself. He must have familiarised himself with her usual routine and made a point of being present when she made her visit to the Smithson cottage.

"It is true, my dear sister, but you have a greater understanding of the economies to which we will be forced, living on a soldier's wages. Mr. Darcy, who has never had a moment of need in his life, is less likely to comprehend the limitations."

"Lord, Lizzy," Lydia said crossly as she brushed away a fly, "I do not see why we must discuss this in the heat and dust of the road. Can we not go to Pemberley House? Or are you too good for your own family now, as Mama says?"

Elizabeth's lips tightened. She had no intention of allowing either of them within a quarter mile of Georgiana, and she did not even wish to imagine what Darcy's response would be to such an appearance.

"Hush, Lydia," Wickham said. "It is not Elizabeth's fault. I am sure Mr. Darcy insists on denying your family, and it is no choice of hers." He smiled at Elizabeth with a good-humoured ease, as if there were an understanding between them.

That there had once been a certain truth in his statement infuriated her yet further. Elizabeth resolved within herself to draw no limits in future to the impudence of an impudent man. "How curious you should think that, since he attended your wedding. But it is no matter. I am sorry I cannot offer you further hospitality."

What had happened to Sylvia? Perhaps she had not understood what Elizabeth wished her to do. She would have to find a way to extract herself from this unfortunate circumstance without Darcy. The challenge lay in how to keep Wickham from embarrassing Darcy with the things he might say to the people of Pemberley, who would not know to disbelieve him.

Wickham took a step closer and spoke in a confidential tone. "I do not wish to put you in a difficult position, my dear sister. But you and I have always understood one another, as I understood your reasons for marrying a man you despised. We all must do what is necessary."

It was one impudence too many, and Elizabeth lost all civility in anger. "Perhaps there was a time when I thought him the last man in the world I could be prevailed upon to marry, but *that* was only when I first knew him, for it is many months since I have considered him the *best* man of my acquaintance. I am astonished to think you might still expect me to share your beliefs now that I have had time to discover the man he truly is and the falseness of your accusations." She forced herself to silence before her loss of control led her to name her brother-in-law a liar and cheat to his face.

To one side, she saw Mrs. Smithson hurrying out of her cottage, her baby on her hip. She grabbed Mr. Wickham's arm and said, "I'll not have you upsetting Mrs. Darcy, George Wickham! I'll not have it! She is the kindest and most generous of ladies. I was willing to take you in for a few days for your mother's sake, but I see you've not changed. Be off with you!" She turned to Elizabeth and dropped a curtsey. "Begging your pardon, madam."

"I see my presence in your defence is quite unnecessary." Darcy's deep voice came from behind Elizabeth.

Startled, she looked over her shoulder at him, expecting to see an expression of distaste or at least dismay, but instead he looked... she did not know quite how to describe it, for he wore his serious look, but underneath it she could see traces of amusement. Certainly he seemed oddly unperturbed by finding her with Wickham.

"Mr. Wickham was just leaving, were you not?" Elizabeth said firmly.

"But Lizzy..." Lydia's pouting expression reminded Elizabeth of the many times she had wheedled concessions from their mother.

With her thoughtless behaviour, Lydia had risked the future of all their sisters, not to mention Elizabeth's new family. A year ago, Elizabeth might have been inclined to continue to treat her as a sister no matter how distasteful her actions, but she was mistress of Pemberley now, with a responsibility to the people of Pemberley and, more importantly, to her husband. She stole a glance at him, then said, "Lydia, if *you* wish to write to me when you reach your new home, I will be glad to read your letters. But your husband is not welcome here, now or ever."

How easy it had been for Wickham to turn her against Darcy when she first knew him! Elizabeth wondered how often the same thing had happened over the years with other acquaintances. No wonder her husband might feel as if no one liked him, if Wickham was behind him at every step so many of those years! And no wonder it had been so easy for him to believe she would never care for him. Suddenly, Wickham's gallantries sickened her.

Mr. Wickham made a courtly bow. "I understand completely, Mrs. Darcy," he said smoothly, with a bit of a smirk towards Darcy. "I take no offence, since I know your character and the necessities you face."

The utter effrontery of the man! And how it must hurt her husband, knowing she had believed Wickham in the past. Just as she had thought the shadows were starting to disappear from his eyes, too. She took a step forward and spoke quietly, so no one would overhear, but made no effort to disguise her anger. "Say one more word against my husband, Mr. Wickham, and I will personally see you horsewhipped."

Finally, she had undercut his presumption; she could see it in his sudden pallor and the way his eyes darted about, as if he knew not how to look. She walked back to Darcy's side and took his arm. "I hope your journey is a pleasant one," she said.

Darcy made a slight bow to them. "Mr. Wickham, Mrs. Wickham." Placing his hand over Elizabeth's, he turned and led her down the lane towards Pemberley House. When they were some distance away, in the shadow of the Pemberley chapel, he looked down at her and raised an eyebrow. "Horsewhipped? Really?"

Elizabeth's cheeks grew hot. "I did not mean you to hear that. But you must admit, he richly deserves it."

"His expression when you said it and when Mrs. Smithson defended you to him was all the revenge I could desire. And I would not have missed it for the world when you called me the *best* man of your acquaintance."

Elizabeth stopped short. "Your hearing is altogether too keen! Although, I do not mind that you heard that, for it is true."

"I appreciate the sentiment, even if I do not believe the substance."

She tilted her head back to smile at him archly. "But it *is* true. You are not, perhaps, the most amiable or complying man of my acquaintance nor even the best-tempered or most eloquent. But the *best* man—that you certainly are. And most exactly the man who in disposition and talents suits me best. Now dispute it if you dare!"

He kissed the tip of her nose. "I dare not dispute anything with you, my love, for if I did the tenants would rush to your defence, throw me off my own lands, and..." He could say no more, since Elizabeth's hand was pressed firmly against his mouth and behind it he was laughing.

"Are you laughing at me, sir?"

He nibbled on her fingertips. "No, I am meditating on the very great distress George Wickham would feel if he knew his machinations had resulted in such a pleasurable outcome for me."

"Because I threatened to have him horsewhipped?"

His expression turned serious. "No, because it was the first time I believed you truly are glad to be married to me, not just making the best of the situation. To hear you defend me so to Wickham, while freely admitting I was once the last man in the world you could be prevailed upon to marry, made *me* the happiest man alive."

"Fitzwilliam! If you have only just realised that, I shall have to add that you are not the cleverest man in the world, since I have felt that way for quite some time and have told you as much. I hope you will believe me now."

"Will you then agree to believe that nothing you say or do will diminish my affection for you?"

Elizabeth pretended to consider the matter. "I doubt it, for I so enjoy the ways you find to reassure me your feelings have not changed. I would be sorry to give those up completely."

He laughed, a full, ringing laugh she had not heard from him before. He picked her up in his arms and kissed her lingeringly, nibbling on her lip.

Suddenly seized by a most peculiar sensation, she pushed against his shoulder. "Fitzwilliam, put me down. Put me down this instant!"

With a worried look, he set her carefully on her feet. "Did I hurt you? I am so very sorry, my love."

She pressed her hands against her waist, half-distracted. "No, no, you did not hurt me. It is quickening!"

He covered her hands with his own. His hands, her hands, and their child.

Elizabeth smiled tremulously. "It is a very strange sensation."

"Come, you must sit down." He led her through the heavy wooden doors into the chapel and helped her into the last pew, where the sun spilled a pool of coloured light from the stained glass window above them.

"I am quite well, you know." She automatically lowered her voice, as she always did in church. There was another odd lurch inside her, as if her stomach had suddenly decided to turn somersaults. A new life. It was humbling and glorious at the same time. She moved closer to Darcy, seeking the comfort of his arm against hers, and looked up to meet his gaze.

He took her hand and pressed it to his lips, making her wedding band glint in the dappled light. How fortunate she was to have him, even if she had struggled to hide her misery the day he put the ring on her finger. So much had changed since then. How she wished she could have it all to do over again, to have begun their marriage in love! But then she might never have come to appreciate her husband's depths the way she did now. Had she never known the despair of losing him, she might never have shared with him some of the deeper secrets of her soul. She had been too private a person for that when she was Miss Elizabeth Bennet of Longbourn. Not even Jane or Charlotte knew as much of her thoughts and fears as her husband did, no matter how their marriage had begun.

She gazed up into Darcy's dark eyes, seeing in them the deep emotion of the moment. Slowly, she spoke the words again, the way she wished she could have spoken them all those months ago, with a full heart. "To have and to hold from this day forward, for better for worse, for richer for poorer, in sickness and in health, to love, cherish, and to obey, till death us do part."

His eyes seemed to encompass all of her as he took in her meaning. Then he replied, "Forsaking all others, as long as we both shall live." He cupped her cheek in his hand and kissed her lightly and decorously, as he had so long ago in the church at Longbourn. "Of course, I meant it the first time I said it, too."

Elizabeth's lips twitched, glad he could tease her about it. "You always were a quick study! I must take my time in considering these matters."

He leaned towards her and spoke quietly in her ear. "I meant the part about 'with my body I thee worship' as well." His tone left little doubt where his thoughts had turned.

"Fitzwilliam! We are in church!" She was half-amused, half-scandalised.

"Then, by all means, let us return to the house." He helped her to her feet and offered her his arm, and together, they emerged into the sunlit lane.

About the Author

ABIGAIL REYNOLDS IS A lifelong Jane Austen enthusiast and a physician. In addition to writing, she has a part-time private practice and enjoys spending time with her family. Originally from upstate New York, she studied Russian, theater, and marine biology before deciding to attend medical school. She began writing *Pride and Prejudice* Variations in 2001 to spend more time with her favorite Jane Austen characters. Encouragement from fellow Austen fans convinced her to continue asking "What if...?" which led to four other *Pride and Prejudice* Variations and her contemporary novel, *The Man Who Loved Pride and Prejudice*. She is currently at work on another Variation and a contemporary sequel. She lives in Wisconsin with her husband, two teenaged children, and a menagerie of pets.

Mr. and Mrs. Fitzwilliam Darcy: Two Shall Become One

SHARON LATHAN

"Highly entertaining... I felt fully immersed in the time period. Well done!" —*Romance Reader at Heart*

A fascinating portrait of a timeless, consuming love

It's Darcy and Elizabeth's wedding day, and the journey is just beginning as Jane Austen's beloved *Pride and Prejudice* characters embark on the greatest adventure of all: marriage and a life together filled with surprising passion, tender self-discovery, and the simple joys of every day.

As their love story unfolds in this most romantic of Jane Austen sequels, Darcy and Elizabeth each reveal to the other how their relationship blossomed from misunderstanding to perfect understanding and harmony, and a marriage filled with romance, sensuality and the beauty of a deep, abiding love.

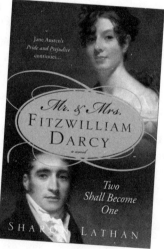

What readers are saying:

"This journey is truly amazing."

"What a wonderful beginning to this truly beautiful marriage."

"Could not stop reading."

"So beautifully written...making me feel as though I was in the room with Lizzy and Darcy...and sharing in all of the touching moments between."

978-1-4022-1523-0 • $14.99 US/ $15.99 CAN/ £7.99 UK

Mr. Darcy Takes a Wife
LINDA BERDOLL
The #1 best-selling Pride and Prejudice sequel

"Wild, bawdy, and utterly enjoyable." —*Booklist*

Hold on to your bonnets!

Every woman wants to be Elizabeth Bennet Darcy—beautiful, gracious, universally admired, strong, daring and outspoken—a thoroughly modern woman in crinolines. And every woman will fall madly in love with Mr. Darcy—tall, dark and handsome, a nobleman and a heartthrob whose virility is matched only by his utter devotion to his wife. Their passion is consuming and idyllic—essentially, they can't keep their hands off each other—through a sweeping tale of adventure and misadventure, human folly and numerous

mysteries of parentage. This sexy, epic, hilarious, poignant and romantic sequel to *Pride and Prejudice* goes far beyond Jane Austen.

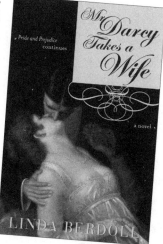

What readers are saying:

"I couldn't put it down."

"I didn't want it to end!"

"Berdoll does Jane Austen proud! ...A thoroughly delightful and engaging book."

"Delicious fun… I thoroughly enjoyed this book."

"My favorite *Pride and Prejudice* sequel so far."

978-1-4022-0273-5 • $16.95 US/ $19.99 CAN/ £9.99 UK

MR. DARCY, VAMPYRE

PRIDE AND PREJUDICE CONTINUES...

AMANDA GRANGE

"A seductively gothic tale..." —Romance Buy the Book

A test of love that will take them to hell and back...

My dearest Jane,

My hand is trembling as I write this letter. My nerves are in tatters and I am so altered that I believe you would not recognise me. The past two months have been a nightmarish whirl of strange and disturbing circumstances, and the future…

Jane, I am afraid.

It was all so different a few short months ago. When I awoke on my wedding morning, I thought myself the happiest woman alive…

"Amanda Grange has crafted a clever homage to the Gothic novels that Jane Austen so enjoyed." —*AustenBlog*

"Compelling, heartbreaking, and triumphant all at once."
—*Bloody Bad Books*

978-1-4022-3697-6
$14.99 US/$18.99 CAN/£7.99 UK

"The romance and mystery in this story melded together perfectly… a real page-turner." —*Night Owl Romance*

"Mr. Darcy makes an inordinately attractive vampire.… *Mr. Darcy, Vampyre* delights lovers of Jane Austen that are looking for more." —*Armchair Interviews*